'Why me?'

'Because you were perfect,' came his smoothly delivered reply.

'Did you mind that I was a virgin?'

'Mind? Why would I have minded?'

She shrugged. 'Because I was inexperienced. I dare say after a while you found me rather boring in bed.'

'Megan, darling. I am being honest. I never thought you boring in bed. At the same time that doesn't mean that I would not have one day moved our love-life in a more... imaginative direction. I get the impression you wouldn't object if I did during our second honeymoon...'

'What do you mean by a more...imaginative direction?'

'I don't think this is the time or place to go into detail. If you trust me, however, as the more experienced partner, I will show you when we get to Dream Island.' His eyes caressed hers in the most seductive fashion.

THREE RICH HUSBANDS

When a wealthy man takes a wife,
it's not always for love…

Meet Russell, Hugh and James,
three wealthy Sydney businessmen who've been
the best of friends for ages. They know each other
very well—including the reasons why none of them
believes in marrying for love.

While Russell and Hugh have so far remained single,
James is about to embark on his second marriage.

But all this is about to change when not just James
but Russell and Hugh too are driven to the altar.
Have any of them changed their minds about love—or
are they ruthlessly making marriages of convenience?

THE BILLIONAIRE'S BRIDE OF VENGEANCE:
Russell's story

THE BILLIONAIRE'S BRIDE OF CONVENIENCE:
Hugh's story

THE BILLIONAIRE'S BRIDE OF INNOCENCE:
James's story

THE BILLIONAIRE'S BRIDE OF INNOCENCE

BY
MIRANDA LEE

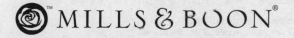

All the characters in this book have no existence outside the imagination
of the author, and have no relation whatsoever to anyone bearing the
same name or names. They are not even distantly inspired by any
individual known or unknown to the author, and all the incidents are
pure invention.

First published in Great Britain 2009
Harlequin Mills & Boon Limited,
Eton House, 18-24 Paradise Road, Richmond, Surrey TW9 1SR

© Miranda Lee 2009

ISBN: 978 0 263 87453 2

Set in Times Roman 10½ on 11½ pt
01-1209-50901

Harlequin Mills & Boon policy is to use papers that are natural,
renewable and recyclable products and made from wood grown in
sustainable forests. The logging and manufacturing process conform
to the legal environmental regulations of the country of origin.

Printed and bound in Spain
by Litografia Rosés, S.A., Barcelona

THE BILLIONAIRE'S BRIDE OF INNOCENCE

PROLOGUE

MEGAN lay on her side in the hard, narrow hospital bed, hoping and praying that the injection the doctor had given her would start working soon. She could not bear to be awake for much longer. Could not bear the pain of her loss for another minute.

Yesterday she had been so happy, the ultrasound showing that she and James were to become the parents of a dear little boy. She'd been over the moon. So had James.

His lovemaking last night had been extra gentle and tender. They'd talked for ages afterwards, discussing what names they would give their son. They'd finally settled on Jonathon, after James's older brother, who'd been tragically killed in a car accident some years earlier.

The cramps had started during the early hours of this morning. Then had come the bleeding. James had rushed her to the hospital and the doctors had done their best. But nothing could save her baby.

Tears flooding her eyes once more, Megan pressed a smothering fist into her trembling mouth when a sob threatened to escape. She didn't want anyone to hear her weeping. She didn't want to listen to any more words of comfort, or sympathy. All she wanted was oblivion. So she bit down on her knuckles and endured her grief in tormented silence.

Time dragged. So did Megan's heart.

Finally, the sedative did its work and she drifted off to sleep. She did not see her husband re-enter the room a short time later. Did not see the distress on his face as he stared down at his sleeping wife. With a sigh he stroked her hair back from her face, then bent to kiss her softly on the cheek. Shaking his head, he straightened then strode from the room.

It was some considerable time before Megan stirred. Even then, her eyes stayed shut, her head feeling thick and heavy. She could hear voices in the room: male voices—gradually she recognised them as belonging to her husband's two best friends.

'James has been out there talking to that doctor for a long time,' Hugh said irritably.

Hugh Parkinson was the only son and heir to a media fortune. Although he was a playboy by reputation, Megan had always found him rather sweet. He'd been best man at her wedding and had made the loveliest of speeches.

'He's probably worried about Megan's condition,' Russell answered. Russell McClain was one of Sydney's most successful real-estate agents.

The three men had been best friends since they'd shared a room at boarding school. And, whilst they had little in common besides their wealth and their love of golf, their friendship had endured for over twenty years. Megan sometimes envied their unconditional affection for each other. She'd never been a girl to make friends easily, being somewhat shy and introverted.

'Huh!' Hugh snorted. 'More likely making sure that she can have more babies.'

Megan was shocked, both by the reproach in Hugh's voice and the inference behind his words. Surely he didn't think James had only married her because she'd been pregnant! That wasn't right. James loved her. She knew he did. Why, he told her so all the time!

'He should never have married that poor girl,' Hugh raved on. 'It was wrong. No, damn it, it was downright wicked. Serve him right if she can't have more kids.'

Megan's mouth fell open. Why was Hugh being so cruel and so condemning of his friend?

'That's a bit harsh, Hugh,' Russell said.

'No, it's not. Marriage should be about true love, not satisfying an egotistical need to reproduce.'

'There's nothing wrong with James wanting a family. It's unfortunate that he doesn't love Megan, but he *is* very fond of her.'

Megan had almost stopped breathing by this stage, the emotional pain of her miscarriage eclipsed by a shock even more devastating than the loss of her baby. She could survive that loss—eventually—if she had her husband's love.

But it seemed she didn't.

Oh, God…

'I could forgive him if the girl had conceived by accident,' Hugh said. 'Marrying her under those circumstances would have been the honourable thing to do. What I find hard to condone is that he deliberately set out to impregnate her first.'

Megan had to stuff her fist into her mouth to stop herself from crying out. It was just as well she had her back to Russell and Hugh or they might have seen her hand move.

'I can understand why he did that,' Russell remarked. 'You must remember what he was like when he found out Jackie was barren. The poor bastard was beside himself.'

Barren! His first wife was *barren*?

James had told her his first marriage had ended because Jackie, an Australian supermodel, wanted a jet-setting lifestyle, whereas he wanted a normal family life. He'd claimed they'd been drifting apart for ages and had split up by mutual consent. It was obvious, however, from what his friends were saying, that James had divorced Jackie because she couldn't have children.

Megan desperately tried to find some mitigating circumstances against such a ruthless course of action. Maybe they *had* been drifting apart. They couldn't have been madly in love, or James would surely have suggested adoption. Unless, of course, he was one of those egotistical men who only wanted a child who carried his own genes. Hugh had implied as much.

'I could forgive the man if he'd chosen a tough bird like Jackie,' Hugh growled. 'But, of course, that wouldn't do the second time round, would it? James had to regain total control of his life. So he zeroed in on an innocent young virgin who was so swept off her feet by the dashing James Logan that she wasn't able to see the wood for the trees.'

'You don't know Megan was a virgin,' Russell pointed out. 'She *is* twenty-four. Not too many twenty-four-year-old virgins around these days.'

'Oh, for pity's sake, Russ, you only have to look at the way she acts around James to know he was her first lover. She's utterly besotted with him. He could tell her the world was flat and she'd believe him.'

Megan cringed, whilst Russell sighed.

'Probably,' he said. 'But that doesn't mean James won't make a good husband and father. He's a bit ruthless at times, but still basically a good man. And a good friend. We have no right to judge him, Hugh, we're far from being perfect. And it's not as though Megan knows the truth.'

'But what if she finds out?'

'Who's going to tell her? Not us, that's for sure.'

No, Megan thought wretchedly. You wouldn't tell me. Not even you, Hugh, who obviously didn't approve of James's actions. Both of you stood up at my wedding and bore witness to James promising to love, honour and cherish me when you knew it was all a lie.

Megan froze when she heard the door open, followed by the sound of her husband's voice.

'Sorry to be so long,' he said to his friends. 'Megan still asleep?'

'Hasn't moved a muscle,' Russell replied. 'What did the doctor say?'

'There's no reason why, in time, Megan can't have another baby. But he cautioned not to rush things. He said it's going to take quite a while for her to get over this. She's taken it very hard.' He sighed a weary sigh. 'We both have. It was a boy, you know,' he went on somewhat croakily. 'We were going to call him Jonathon…'

Megan hated hearing the distress in her husband's voice. Hated the fact that she could still sympathise with his pain.

'I'm sorry, mate,' Hugh said, all condemnation clearly gone now. 'We do know how much having children means to you. You must be feeling really rotten. Come on, we'll take you for a drink. There's a pub just down the road.'

'I'll have to check on Megan first.'

'Sure thing.'

Megan felt the warmth of his breath on her cheek as he bent over her.

'Megan, darling, can you hear me?'

Why, oh, why did she open her eyes?

'How are you feeling?' he asked her gently.

Her eyes filled with tears as she stared up into the face of the man she loved, and who she'd thought loved her.

'Go away,' she choked out. 'Please…just go away!' The sobs came in earnest then, shoulder-wracking, heartbreaking sobs. She simply could not stop.

'I'll get the nurse,' he said.

The nurse hurried in, a kind, motherly creature who took Megan in her arms and just held her.

'There, there, dear,' she crooned. 'I know how you feel. I lost a baby once.'

But I've lost more than that, Megan agonised. I've lost everything!

And she sobbed all the louder.

'Best leave her for now,' the nurse directed at James, who was obviously hovering near by. 'I'll get the doctor to give her something stronger. She'll be out of it for some time. Come back this evening. Hopefully, she'll be feeling better by then.'

No, I won't, Megan thought despairingly. I'm never going to feel better. Never!

CHAPTER ONE

Three months later…

SYDNEY in late April often belied the fact that winter was just over a month away. The nights and mornings could be crisp, but the days were usually warm and rain-free, the skies clear and blue.

The day of Hugh's wedding was such a day. By mid-afternoon the temperature had reached a very pleasant twenty-four degrees, which was just as well, since Megan had little in the way of warm outfits to choose from in her wardrobe. She hadn't been clothes shopping since she'd come home from hospital in January. In actual fact, she hadn't been out of the house.

Till now…

Megan sat stiffly, her handsome husband beside her, in the second row of seats which had been set up on the main deck of the father of the groom's super-yacht. When the invitation had first arrived, she'd immediately declined to attend. But James had said he wouldn't go if she didn't come with him. Then Hugh had called personally to ask her to reconsider. It wasn't going to be a big wedding, he'd assured her. Only sixty or so guests.

'It will do you good to get out,' he'd argued. 'You can't go on like this, Megan.'

Which was true, of course. She couldn't continue living the way she had, shutting the world out, shutting everyone out. Especially James. She had to make a decision whether to leave him or not, a decision which seemed beyond her. Making any decision seemed beyond her. The only way she made it through each day was by absorbing herself in the one activity she could rely on to provide some escape from the conflicting emotions which constantly besieged her mind.

Painting had always been an all-consuming passion for her, even when she was quite young. As a teenager she'd dreamt of becoming a famous artist one day, of having her works hung in the finest galleries in Australia. She'd begged her father to send her to art school after she'd graduated from high school and, much to her mother's disgust, he'd agreed.

Megan had spent three years honing her craft, receiving much critical acclaim from her teachers, but not from the art world at large. She'd only ever had one painting exhibited— in a small gallery in Bondi—so it seemed unlikely she would ever achieve the level of success she'd once craved.

But she'd kept on painting, even after she'd married James, though it had been relegated to more of a hobby by then.

Now it was her one and only survival weapon, a way of coping.

It was ironic that, if James ever saw the canvas she'd been working on since her miscarriage, he would sweep her back to the doctor who'd diagnosed her with depression a few days after her miscarriage. No doubt he'd give her another prescription of anti-depressants, along with some more sleeping tablets.

As if pills could fix her problem!

Nothing could fix her problem but herself. Deep down, Megan had always known that. She'd finally thrown all the pills away a few weeks ago and hadn't felt any worse. In fact, surprisingly, she'd begun to feel a bit better.

Deciding to leave the house and go to Hugh's wedding was still a huge step for her, but she made it.

So here she was, dressed in the pale pink suit which had been her own going-away outfit, and which was now a size too large. She'd had to move the button on the waistband over to make sure the skirt stayed put. The jacket was a bit loose, but that was all right. It had once been somewhat snug. Her long dark hair was caught up in a French roll. She hadn't been to a hairdresser in ages and this was the only sophisticated style which she could manage herself. Her make-up had taken her ages: foundation, lipstick and blusher to counter the pallor of her skin and lots of eye make-up, using toning shades of eyeshadow to complement her brown eyes and heaps of mascara. No eyeliner, however. She had tried it but her hands had trembled and she'd poked herself in the eye, making it water, so she gave up on that idea.

James had said she looked lovely when he'd first seen her today.

Inside, she'd shrunk from his compliment, in much the same way that she shrank from him whenever he tried to show affection to her. This time, however, she'd managed a small smile and a polite thank-you. Then, when he'd taken her hand as they walked up the gangway onto the yacht, she hadn't snatched it away. She'd left it there.

That had been a mistake, Megan now realised as she stared down at where James still had her hand clasped firmly within his. Hand-holding might not be all that intimate an activity, but it was closer than anything Megan had allowed since her miscarriage.

Not once since she'd come home from hospital had Megan let James make love to her. Frankly, the idea of going to bed with him made her feel ill. Whenever he tried to take her into his arms she'd pull away with a sharp 'no!', after which she would usually make some pathetic excuse, saying that she was sorry, that she just couldn't. Not yet.

He'd been amazingly patient with her, but she wasn't a complete fool. She'd glimpsed the frustration on his face at times, had seen it increasing over the last month. He'd started working longer and longer hours, probably so that he didn't have to be home with a wife who rejected him all the time. And she'd started spending more and more time down in her studio, painting. Sometimes she even slept down there.

Her letting James hold her hand might not seem like a big deal, but Megan could see that her husband was looking pretty pleased with himself just now. Pleased with her, too. He was sure to try to make love to her again tonight and he would be expecting her not to reject him this time.

The music started up—the traditional *Bridal March*—James's fingers tightening around Megan's as he pulled her to her feet. Their eyes met briefly, Megan startled by the sudden lurching of her stomach. She quickly looked away before he could see the shock in her face.

That couldn't have been a spark of desire she'd just experienced, could it?

How perverse if it was. Wickedly perverse.

She didn't want to want him. Ever again.

But if Megan was brutally honest with herself, this was what she'd been fearing all along, that, if she didn't leave James, one day he would succeed in seducing her again. That was why she'd avoided all physical contact. And why she'd gone on the Pill. Because she'd known, deep down, that she was still vulnerable to her husband's prowess in the bedroom.

Sex with James had far surpassed anything she'd ever dreamt about. Had from the word go, despite her virginity, and she'd simply thought him wonderful.

She'd thought him even more wonderful on their honeymoon. She'd been suffering a slight case of morning sickness during their two weeks in Hawaii and he couldn't have been more considerate.

But when James had been away on business during the

weeks leading up to their wedding, Megan had experienced a taste of what frustration was like. Memories of his expert lovemaking had tormented her every night during his absence, and she'd lain awake for hours as she'd relived every exciting moment.

By the time their wedding night had come around, she'd wanted him like crazy. She'd wallowed in their seemingly mutual passion that night, and had been upset when her nausea each morning had interrupted their lovemaking. She'd been looking forward to spending long hours every day in his arms. As it was, James had still made love to her each evening, and occasionally in the middle of the night as well, before her morning nausea kicked in.

By the time they'd returned from their honeymoon, Megan had become used to being made love to at least once a day. When James went back to work, however, their sex life had lessened somewhat. Megan had thought this was because James was tired. As the owner of one of Sydney's most successful advertising agencies, he worked very hard. She realised now that he was probably bored with her. His mission had been accomplished, after all: she had been carrying his child and was blindly besotted with him.

She supposed it *was* possible that he thought she wouldn't want him as much, once she became pregnant. Just the opposite was the case, however. She'd wanted James more than ever.

There'd been a few times when Megan was so frustrated that she thought of initiating things herself. Once, when they'd been swimming in the pool together on a hot summer night. Another time, when they'd been getting ready to go out on New Year's Eve. James had been in the shower, whistling, and she'd suddenly been tempted to strip off and join him. She'd experienced a strong urge to do some of the things to him that she'd read about in books: bold, sexy things, with her hands and her mouth.

But, in the end, she hadn't had the confidence.

Still, her desire for her husband, Megan now understood, had always been far greater than his desire for her. Which was only natural; she *loved* him.

She still loved him, despite everything. Loved him and, to her shock and shame today, still wanted him.

Where, in heaven's name, was her pride?

Not much in evidence at that moment, her heartbeat quickening when he turned to her and smiled one of those supersexy smiles which had used to turn her to mush.

In desperation, she managed to extricate her hand with the excuse that she always cried at weddings and needed to get a tissue from her handbag.

'I have to admit,' James said as she rifled through her handbag, 'that I never thought this day would come. Hugh always vowed and declared that he would never get married.'

Megan recalled what she'd overheard Hugh saying at the hospital; that marriage should be the result of true love, and nothing else.

'Still, I have a feeling he'll be more successful at marriage than his father,' James whispered to her. 'Not that that'd be hard. I've lost count of how many wives Dickie Parkinson has had, each one younger than the last. Hugh's chosen very well, I think. Kathryn's a lovely girl. And very sensible. Oh, wow!' he exclaimed. 'What is it about brides that means they always look absolutely gorgeous?'

Megan was glad to have something to distract herself from the turmoil in her heart, her head turning to watch the bride walk down the aisle.

Megan didn't know much about Kathryn Hart, only that she'd been Hugh's PA. But James was right. She made an absolutely beautiful bride, dressed in a strapless white gown which had a tight beaded bodice and a gathered floor-length skirt. It was very similar in style to her own wedding gown, though hers had been ivory, not white. Kathryn seemed to float down the strip of red carpet which bisected the rows of seats, a long tulle veil trailing after her, her dark hair up and anchored in place by a tiara of white roses.

Megan's eyes swung back to where the minister was standing along with Hugh and Russell, both looking resplendent in black dinner suits, white roses in their lapels. As handsome as both men were, neither of them could hold a candle to James, in her opinion.

Her eyes slid surreptitiously back to her husband, whose attention, thankfully, was elsewhere.

There was no doubt James was a striking-looking man: very tall and well-built, with a masculine face and deep-set, extremely dark eyes that commanded immediate attention. His cheekbones were prominent, his nose strong and straight, his mouth nicely shaped. His ears sat flat against his well-shaped head, which was just as well, because he always wore his dark brown hair very short, giving a tough-guy edge to his otherwise conservative image.

Women would still have thrown themselves at him, Megan conceded, even if he hadn't been rich and powerful.

On top of that, he was always superbly dressed. The white-jacketed dinner suit he was wearing today was no off-the-peg variety. It had been tailored especially to fit him. But he looked just as good without clothes, she knew, his shoulders naturally broad and his muscles well honed from regular workouts in the gym. His quite magnificent male body was well-equipped to satisfy a woman in every way.

He satisfied me, she recalled. Every time.

And he'd satisfy you again, a devilish voice piped up in her head. All you have to do is let him…

Her face flushed at the temptation, a small groan escaping her lips.

When James's head whipped round, she brought the tissue up to her mouth and tried not to look embarrassed.

'You're not crying already, are you?' he said, but with an indulgent little smile.

'Not yet,' she croaked out.

'You are a real softie, aren't you? But I love that about you.'

Do you? she wondered as she wrenched her eyes away from his. Do you actually love *anything* about me?

Russell had said he was fond of her. That could be true, Megan conceded. James was always very nice to her.

But being fond of someone was a wishy-washy, lukewarm feeling, no match for the mad passion James had evoked in her from the start, and which she'd believed was mutual. How much of his so-called passion on their wedding night had been pretend? Did he have any real desire for her? Or was she just a means to an end?

Megan was well aware that men could not fake an erection. But it didn't take much for a man in his prime—and James, at thirty-six, was still a young man—to become aroused. It was a well-known fact that men didn't need love to want to have sex; just a willing woman in most cases.

She'd been very willing. And very naïve.

But not so naïve any longer.

If she ever went to bed with James again, she would have to do so with the full knowledge that he didn't love her.

Could she do that? Could she really?

Before today, she would have said no. Definitely not!

Now she wasn't quite so sure…

'I hope Russell hasn't forgotten the rings,' James said. 'We don't want any dramas like we had at his wedding. Remember how that dreadful mother of Nicole's showed up at the last minute and accused him of marrying her daughter for revenge?'

'Yes, I remember,' Megan said tautly.

'Stupid woman. As if any man would marry for revenge. Anyone with half a brain could see that Russell was madly in love.'

Megan glanced at Russell, who was right at that moment smiling at Nicole, who'd preceded the bride down the aisle and looked absolutely exquisite in pale green. Megan recalled their wedding very well; recalled actually standing up and clapping when Nicole had said love was all that mattered. Megan had not long been back from her honeymoon at the time, her blind belief in James's love having given her a new confidence and self-esteem, all of which had vanished the day she'd lost her baby boy. And, with it, her innocence.

James's low chuckle dragged her back to the present. 'Poor Hugh,' he said. 'If that look on his face is anything to go by, then Kathryn is going to run rings around him.'

Megan stared at Hugh as he stared at his bride, his expression one of total adoration and admiration. His eyes even filled with tears as she drew close.

That's what *I* want, she thought, her heart squeezing tight. For James to look at me like that. For him to really truly love me.

But that wasn't going to happen, was it? came the voice of brutal honesty. And you're never going to leave him. Not now that you want him again.

Megan had never imagined that she would actually cry. She'd been beyond tears for some time now. But suddenly, there they were, flooding her eyes, her one single tissue totally inadequate to mop up the flood.

James came to the rescue with a clean white handkerchief before putting a tender arm around her shoulders.

'What a silly billy you are,' he said gently. 'Weddings are happy occasions, not sad.'

'I…I want to go home,' she cried. 'Please take me home.'

James sighed. 'I can't, Megan. Not yet. Look, I promise we won't stay late but I can't just up and leave. Hugh is one of my best friends. You know that.'

The arrival overhead of a helicopter hired by the media drowned out the rest of her weeping. Fortunately, it didn't come low enough to ruin hairdos and blow hats off, but it was still quite noisy, the minister having to talk louder and louder. The helicopter finally left just after Hugh and Kathryn were pronounced man and wife, by which time Megan had stopped crying. But the release of emotion had left her feeling totally drained.

She only just managed to get through the next few hours, though she did hide in one of the luxurious powder rooms for a while. Megan had always found making idle conversation difficult when faced with people she didn't know, which meant most of the guests at this wedding. There was also a measure of guilt when faced with the few people she did know, especially Russell and Nicole. She felt terrible that she'd rejected all of their social invitations over the last few months, and never invited them back.

More guilt followed when they were so nice to her.

And all the while she was cripplingly aware of James, and the physical effect he was suddenly having on her. Even when he wasn't by her side, she found herself watching him. Jealousy raised its ugly head whenever she saw him chatting to other women—*attractive* women.

It came to her suddenly that maybe her handsome husband—the one who didn't love her—might not have been as frustrated as she'd imagined these past three months. Maybe he hadn't been working when he came home so late every other night. Maybe he'd been having sex with one or more of the many beautiful women whom he met on a daily basis. Running an advertising and management agency brought him into constant contact with actresses and models, most of them beautiful and glamorous, all of them sophisticated women-of-the-world. He wouldn't have any trouble finding a casual bed-partner.

When James finally said his goodbyes to the happy couple, Megan was more than ready to leave, her jealousy by then bubbling up inside her like a rumbling volcano.

She wanted to erupt, wanted to throw angry accusations at him. Wanted to tell him that she knew he didn't love her, that he'd only married her to have children. She wanted to start a fight.

She almost did. They'd stopped at a set of traffic lights and she actually turned towards him, her mouth opening to launch into her tirade.

If only James hadn't chosen that moment to bend over and kiss her. Not sweetly but hungrily, his right hand cupping her chin, keeping her mouth captive beneath his onslaught.

If Megan had been in any doubt earlier that her desire for James had been well and truly revived, then his kiss quickly cemented that realisation. The kiss went on and on, James's head only lifting when the car behind them beeped impatiently.

'Keep your skirt on,' he muttered, his mouth still hovering close to her lips. 'I'm busy, kissing my wife.' And then he kissed her again, ignoring the now blaring horn, ignoring the other driver's verbal abuse as he was forced to angle past their still stationary vehicle.

By the time James stopped kissing her, Megan's volcanic anger had been replaced by a desire so intense that it threatened what was left of her sanity. This was even worse than she'd feared, much worse. This wasn't just wanting to be made love to. This was a craving so strong that it would not be denied.

Her skin crawled with the need to be touched. Her body ached to be filled. At that moment nothing else mattered. Not the fact that he didn't love her, or that he'd probably been unfaithful.

Thank goodness that she'd had the forethought to go on the Pill!

When more cars started to honk their horns at them, James sighed and turned his attention back to the steering wheel.

The drive home saved her. Or was it the last vestiges of her pride that came to the rescue? Whatever, by the time James went through the gates of the six-bedroom mansion he'd bought shortly after their marriage, Megan had managed to get some control over her treacherously weak flesh.

'Do you fancy a nightcap?' James asked as they both climbed out of his car.

'No, nothing,' Megan replied quickly. 'The thing is, James, I have this terrible headache. I'm going to take some tablets and go straight up to bed.'

He stared at her over the bonnet of the car, his dark eyes not happy. 'A headache,' he said slowly.

Megan didn't say a word.

'You do realise this can't continue, Megan.'

'Yes,' she replied tautly, then looked away from his probing gaze.

'We'll talk in the morning. Before I go to work. Make some decisions about our future.'

Her eyes flew back to his. Maybe he was going to make it easy for her and ask for a divorce himself. Maybe he'd finally lost patience with her. Part of her hoped so.

But not the part which tormented her for hours that night as she lay in their marital bed, her back to James, pretending to be asleep when all the while she was wide-awake.

In the end she could bear it no longer. Rising quietly, she drew the matching silk robe over her nightie and made her way downstairs and out onto the back terrace. The moon was up, moonlight dancing on the water of the swimming pool as she hurried past it down to her studio, shivering in the cool night air as she went.

Once inside what had once been the pool house, she turned on the lights and the air-conditioning and made her way over to the easel that was set up under the skylight which James had had put in for her. Lifting the dust sheet off the canvas, she studied the painting she'd been working on for ages.

It was not what she wanted to work on tonight. Tonight, she would work on something very different indeed.

Quickly she replaced the canvas with an empty one, hiding the other painting in a cupboard. After that, she sat down on the stool in front of the easel and began to mix her paints, every now and then glancing up at herself in the long mirror which hung on the wall opposite.

Could she capture that look on canvas? she wondered.

What did it matter if she couldn't? No one would ever see this painting, or the other one, but herself.

CHAPTER TWO

JAMES emerged from the bathroom and stood there for a long moment, glowering at the king-sized bed which dominated the elegantly furnished master bedroom and which, at that moment, looked as if it had been in the path of a herd of stampeding elephants.

The dishevelled state of the sheets and pillows wasn't the result of a night of satisfying lovemaking with his wife, something he'd been hoping for when he'd kissed her in the car last night and she'd responded like the Megan of old.

Instead, the moment they arrived home from Hugh's wedding, she'd claimed a headache and bolted for bed straight away, although it hadn't been late, only about eight-thirty. Then, soon after he'd finally come to bed around eleven, she'd upped and fled the room altogether, leaving him to toss and turn, the meagre hours of sleep he'd managed to get being peppered with darkly erotic, highly arousing dreams. He'd woken this morning and even after a fifteen-minute cold shower he'd felt extremely frustrated.

Tightening his tie, James marched across the plush cream carpet and flung open the French doors which led out onto the sun-drenched balcony. Dark brows bunched together, he gripped the curved railing top and peered down at the pool house which sat at the far end of the swimming pool.

He couldn't see inside the pool house. But he knew she was in there, painting.

When he'd had the pool house converted into an art studio for Megan, James had imagined he was doing the right thing, giving his emotionally fragile young wife something to distract her from her grief. She'd taken losing their baby very hard, even harder than he had.

James had never anticipated that she would end up spending all day, every day in there—and now every other night as well.

What he'd thought might be good therapy had become an obsession. Hell, she wouldn't even let him look at any of her work. Goodness knew why. She didn't seem to want to share any part of her life with him any more. It was the bed part, however, which bothered James the most.

Megan's doctor had said to be patient; that Megan was an especially sensitive young woman; that he couldn't expect her to want sex for a little while.

Well, he'd been more than patient in his opinion, and a 'little while' had turned into three long months. James had coped. *Just.* What he could not cope with was the constant delay in trying for another child. He was already thirty-six years old, older than he'd planned to be when he became a father.

Becoming a dad was what James wanted most in the world these days, but it was almost impossible if your wife never let you make love to her.

James sympathised with Megan. He really did. But running away from life was no answer. You had to face up to things, then move on.

Of course, Megan was an extremely soft, shy, vulnerable girl. That was why he'd chosen her.

Because she was nothing like Jackie.

James's heart twisted when he thought of his first wife. Why was it that men often fell for the wrong woman?

Jackie had captivated him from the start, his mad passion for her beautiful body blinding him to her materialistic motives in marrying him. The ugly truth had been outed when she'd been unable to conceive and James had suggested IVF, or adoption. When she'd rejected both of his suggestions out of hand, James began to suspect that Jackie didn't want children at all. During the course of their subsequent argument, she admitted that she'd known all along that she was infertile, that she could never give him the family he so desired.

That she hadn't really loved him had also become obvious to James. He'd just been a ticket to the good life, an insurance policy for the future when her modelling life came to an end.

What she'd done had been wicked, and cruel, and totally selfish.

Hugh and Russell believed he was still in love with Jackie.

But he wasn't. She'd killed his love for her. Unfortunately, it seemed she'd also killed his ability to fall in love again. As much as he wanted to be in love with Megan, James knew he wasn't. He liked her very much, though, and he liked making love to her.

Or he *had*.

Of course, sex with Megan wasn't as exciting as it had been with Jackie. How could it be? Jackie had been an experienced woman-of-the-world with lots of tricks to turn a guy on. Megan had been a virgin when James had met her, shy and somewhat inhibited. Total nudity still embarrassed her, so their sex life so far—when they'd had one!—had been pretty conservative, with James always the initiator.

Not that she wasn't a passionate girl, she was. Right from the start James had received surprising satisfaction in Megan's obvious pleasure in his lovemaking.

In hindsight, he wasn't at all sure about Jackie. Faking it would have been part of her modus operandi.

Nothing fake about Megan, or her love for him. James knew that.

Occasionally, he did experience some momentary guilt that he didn't love her back; usually when Hugh and Russell made some uncomplimentary remark on the subject. Or sometimes, when he told her that he loved her. But whenever that happened, logic soon came to the rescue. Megan didn't know he didn't love her and James firmly believed he could make her happy.

If she'd only let him...

Frustration on several levels sent him striding back into the bedroom, where he slipped into his suit jacket, then collected his wallet and mobile phone from the bedside table. With one last glower at the messy bed, he headed downstairs, where the enticing smell of freshly brewed coffee indicated that his breakfast was almost ready.

'Good morning, Mr Logan,' Roberta said cheerily when he walked into the kitchen. 'Your breakfast won't be long.'

As housekeepers went, Roberta was a gem. James had hired her shortly after he'd bought this place from Russell late last year, knowing that the huge Bellevue Hill mansion was way too large for Megan to look after by herself. Though in her mid-fifties, Roberta was still slim and very fit, and a simply wonderful cook. Her handyman husband coming with the deal was a bonus. Running Images left James with little time for gardening, or cleaning the pool.

Even so, James had every intention of semi-retiring once his first child was born. When he'd come to the decision a few years back to embrace fatherhood rather than run away from it, James had resolved to give being a parent one hundred and ten per cent effort.

His own father's pathetic example had shown him what not to do. James didn't want any son—or daughter—of his to feel what he'd felt when he'd been growing up. No way!

'Could you hold breakfast for a while this morning,

Roberta? I'm going to pop down to the pool house for a few minutes.'

Roberta shook her head sadly. 'Mrs Logan spent the night painting again, did she?'

James hesitated. Since his ego-bruising break-up with Jackie, James had become a bit paranoid about keeping his private life…private. But it was difficult to keep secrets around Roberta. She was a canny woman—though, thankfully, a kind one.

'Afraid so,' he admitted.

'Poor love. I've tried talking to her, you know. Told her that lots of miscarriages are nature's way when something isn't quite right.'

'And?'

Roberta shrugged. 'She said she already knew that.'

James nodded. Yes. The doctor would have explained that to her, since he'd told him the same thing, reassuring James that there was no reason why his wife's next pregnancy wouldn't be fine.

'I've decided to take Megan away on a second honeymoon,' James informed Roberta. 'Get her right away from here, and that infernal studio.'

'That's a very good idea. She can't keep going on the way she is. She's living on her nerves. And she eats like a bird. I can't remember the last day she had a proper breakfast. Or lunch, for that matter.'

James frowned. He'd noticed her picking at her meal at night, but hadn't realised she wasn't eating much during the day, either.

'Why don't you make up a breakfast tray for two, Roberta, and I'll take it down with me? That way I can sit with her and make sure she eats something.'

'That's another good idea. It shouldn't take me too long.'

'I'll get myself a cup of that great coffee of yours while I wait.'

Ten minutes later, James arrived at the pool house with a well-stocked breakfast tray in his hands. The door was closed, James knocking with the toe of his shoe.

'It's me, Megan,' he called out at the same time. 'Can you open the door for me? My hands are full.'

The door eventually opened, with a sleepy-eyed Megan half hiding behind it.

'What time is it?' she asked.

'Breakfast time,' he answered, and walked in with the tray, putting it down on the small round table which sat to the right of the door. When he pulled out a chair for her, Megan ignored it. Instead, she hurried over to the easel, where she threw a dust sheet over the canvas, then sat down on her stool and started cleaning her brushes.

'How's the painting coming along?' he said, suppressing his irritation with difficulty.

'Fine,' Megan said without looking up.

'Am I going to be allowed to see it one day?'

'Not till it's finished,' she said, still not looking his way.

Megan had confessed to him early on in their relationship that she had a dream of becoming a famous artist, an ambition which James never believed would come to fruition, mainly because he didn't think she had enough talent. Megan was a good painter; she hadn't spent several years at art school for nothing. But her paintings simply didn't have that special something which made them stand out from the crowd.

They'd met last year at an art gallery, in front of the one and only painting of Megan's ever to be exhibited. It hadn't been to his taste—he'd never liked still-life pictures—but he'd bought it anyway at the end of the evening, knowing by then that he'd found the ideal girl to marry. Attractive enough and suitably young, with a sweetly innocent way about her which always appealed to cynical men-of-the-world. That she also came from a well-off family hadn't hurt, either, James not wanting to risk marrying a gold-digger again.

He'd encouraged her to keep on painting after their marriage, thinking it would be good for her to have an involving hobby. He'd certainly encouraged her to keep on painting after her miscarriage, even putting up with her suddenly developing the kind of artistic temperament which didn't allow anyone to see what she was working on whilst the work was in progress.

But there was a limit to his patience, and he was fast reaching the end of it!

'Roberta tells me you haven't been eating breakfast,' he said somewhat sharply.

Now she glanced over at him, her eyes startled, perhaps by his harsh tone. Megan's big brown eyes were very expressive.

'I…I haven't been very hungry lately,' she said, and turned her attention back to her brushes.

'Come and have some juice, then.'

'In a moment…'

James counted to ten before saying firmly, 'Megan. We have to talk.'

'Yes, you're right,' she said. 'We do.' But she made no move to join him at the table.

His patience finally ran out.

'Then have the decency to stop what you're doing and come over here!' he snapped before he could stop himself.

He hated himself immediately for taking that tone with her. But, truly, there was a limit to what he could endure.

He watched, somewhat chastened, as she put down her brushes, stood up, then re-sashed her silk robe tightly around her waist, bringing his attention to just how much weight she'd lost since her miscarriage.

When he'd first met Megan, she'd been nothing out of the

ordinary, a reasonably pretty, round-faced brunette with nice eyes, a few too many pounds and not much interest in how she presented herself. Like a lot of people with an artistic bent, she was introverted and unworldly. By the time he'd married her two months later, however, she'd smartened herself up considerably, admitting later that she'd sought the help of a professional style guru who'd helped her with her wedding dress and her honeymoon wardrobe, then shown her how to do herself up to her best advantage.

James had been taken aback—and turned on—by the more sophisticated look of his bride when he first saw her on their wedding day, having been overseas on business during the weeks leading up to their marriage. Her bridal gown was a delight, the strapless style and corset-like bodice giving her body a sexy, hourglass shape.

James hadn't given Jackie a second thought on his wedding night. Quite a feat after running into his first wife in New York three days earlier, on the arm of her latest lover.

He wasn't thinking of Jackie now, either, his eyes—and his concentration—totally on Megan as she turned and moved towards him.

Yesterday, at Hugh's wedding, he'd thought she looked very attractive. Today, however, she looked seriously sexy and quite beautiful. Yet she wasn't wearing any make-up and her hair wasn't done properly, just bundled up on top of her head in a decidedly haphazard fashion, with bits and pieces falling down around her face.

The loss of weight suited her, James realised. She now had cheekbones, her eyes looked bigger, her neck looked longer. So did her legs. In fact her whole figure was leaner, but still shapely, with good child-bearing hips, nice breasts and nipples just made for a baby's mouth.

And for a man's.

As James stared at the provocative outline that her nipples

were making against the thin silk of her white negligee, he resolved that last night would be the last time Megan would sleep down here.

Tonight, she would stay in the marital bed.

Tonight, she would *not* turn away from him!

CHAPTER THREE

MEGAN tried to ignore the direction of her husband's coal-black eyes. Tried not to respond to the obvious glitter of desire in their depths.

But it was impossible.

Her nipples tightened, so did her belly, her weakness where he was concerned both exciting and annoying. It was wicked, the way he could affect her. She should have hated him for what he'd done to her. She did hate him. Sometimes.

Don't look at him, she lectured herself. Sit down and pour yourself some juice and simply don't look at him!

He was ahead of her, however, reaching for the jug before she had a chance and pouring the juice for her. She was forced to meet his eyes when he handed the glass over, his expression having changed by then from one of frustration to kind consideration.

'Drink this up, there's a good girl,' he said with one of those warm, winning smiles of his, the kind he reserved for difficult clients. And weak-willed wives.

Still, he wouldn't be calling her a good girl if he looked at the painting she'd worked on all night, Megan thought with bitter irony as she lifted the glass to her lips,

'I've decided to take you away on a second honeymoon,' he said after pouring himself some juice as well.

Megan blinked at him. He'd decided, had he? Just like that.

She had to admire him. At least he could do that—make decisions. Unlike her own wishy-washy self.

'I was talking to Rafe the other day,' he went on, clearly assuming by her silence—and possibly because of the way she'd kissed him yesterday—that she was going to agree. 'You know Rafe, don't you? Rafe Saint Vincent, the photographer. Anyway, he was telling me about this island he went to once, Dream Island. It's off the coast of Queensland up near Cairns. He said it was the perfect place for a romantic getaway; a tropical paradise which offers total privacy and all the luxury in the world.'

Megan's breathing quickened as she imagined what it would be like to go to such a place with James on a second honeymoon. He would be oh, so attentive to her, attentive and loving. And he'd make love to her as passionately and as often as he had when they'd first met.

Because he had a new mission: to make her pregnant again.

It was tempting. There was no doubt about it.

Lots of women in her position would take what he was offering and go on ignoring his lies. They would even try to have another child.

But Megan couldn't do that last part. Not yet. Maybe not ever.

So what *are* you going to do? demanded the voice of reason. The time has come to make a decision. But which one?

Decision one: you confront James with the truth at long last and tell him what you overheard at the hospital. But, of course, if you do that then your marriage is over. You will have no alternative but to go home to your overbearing and critical mother.

Megan shuddered inside at such a prospect.

Decision two: you decide to live with James's lies and give your marriage a second chance. You go on your second honeymoon and enjoy what your husband has to offer you. But you stay on the Pill till you feel ready to have another baby. Naturally, you don't tell him you're taking contraception because, if you do, your marriage will be over and you'll be back home with Mother again.

It really was a no-brainer, not the way she was feeling right at this moment. She had to experience his lovemaking at least one more time, or go crazy.

'That sounds…nice,' she heard herself saying.

'Darling,' he murmured, reaching over to take her hand in his. 'I can't tell you how happy you've just made me. I've missed you terribly in bed,' he said, stroking her fingers all the while. 'You must know that.'

Suddenly, and perhaps perversely, she found the courage to at least give voice to one of her concerns. 'Actually no, James,' she choked out, even as her stomach contracted into a savage knot of desire. 'I don't know that.'

His eyes betrayed true surprise, his fingers stilling on hers. 'What do you mean?'

'You are the big boss of Images; a very rich, very powerful man. If you'd wanted sex these past few months, you'd have had no trouble getting it.'

There was no doubting his shock. Either that, or he was the best actor in the world.

'I have never been unfaithful to you, Megan. Never! I want you and only you,' he insisted, lifting her curled-over hand to his lips and kissing her knuckles.

It was probably a lie, Megan thought dazedly. But a brilliant one. She could perhaps live with lies like that, if he kept delivering them with such seeming sincerity, along with some of his exquisite lovemaking.

'I'll get right on to booking a place on Dream Island as soon as I get to work,' he continued with his usual decisiveness. 'But before I leave, can I tempt you with some cereal? Or a croissant?'

'Not just now,' she said tersely, and pulled her hand out of his hold.

James frowned as only James could, his thick dark brows beetling together, his black eyes glittering with instant disapproval. 'As much as you're looking incredibly lovely today, my darling, you don't want to lose any more weight. Not if we're going to try for another baby.'

Her nostrils sucked in sharply before she could stop them.

'Is there a problem with that?' he demanded to know straight away. 'Is it still too soon for you?'

A hundred years would be too soon, she wanted to scream at him. Oh, God, what if she never wanted to have another baby? What if this fear never passed?

'The doctor said there was no physical reason for you to have another miscarriage,' James went on before she could find the right reply. 'Look, you said when we married that you wanted a big family.'

'Yes, I know I did,' she said tightly. And she still *did*!

It was all so impossible, Megan realised despairingly.

'Tell me what's bothering you,' he persisted.

'I can't.'

'You can, you know,' he said, reaching over and touching her hand again. 'You can tell me anything. Would it help if I said I already know what it is?'

Megan snatched her hand away from under his. He *knew* she didn't want to have a baby? Knew she was on the Pill?

'You think you don't want sex any more,' he pronounced baldly as he sat back in his chair.

Megan almost laughed, just managing to hide her reaction by looking away and picking up her orange juice.

Any secret amusement—however perverse—was soon squashed when he rose abruptly from his chair and strode round to hers. Megan froze whilst he swept the glass of juice from her hand and banged it back onto the tray. Two seconds later, her chair had been twisted away from the table and he was pulling her up into his arms.

'I should have done this last night,' he growled as his mouth swooped.

Megan didn't want him to kiss her, not right now!

But there was no stopping him.

She tried not to respond but it was a futile struggle from the start. Her mind quickly dissolved, along with her body. There was no thought of resistance. There was nothing but blind acceptance that this was where she wanted to be. In his arms. She forgot, in the heat of the moment, that her period had arrived just before dawn that morning...

CHAPTER FOUR

YES!

A wild elation swept through James when Megan finally responded. For a moment there, he'd thought she was going to reject him again.

But there was no rejection in the way she was suddenly pressing herself against him.

God, but he'd really missed her. Missed this.

She was so sweet, he thought as his mouth softened against hers. Delicious, really. His mind was already racing ahead of his actions, thinking of how for once he would make love to her out of a bed and in broad daylight. Soon he'd pick her up and carry her over to the red leather sofa under the window. Soon he'd be inside her.

First, however, he would have to get her a little more excited, or she might object. She really was incredibly shy.

He lifted his mouth from hers but he didn't let her go, turning her round in his arms so that her back was against him. His left arm wound tightly around her waist, his right hand left free. Free to slide into the neckline of her robe and cup her breast, playing with her nipple through the thin silk of her nightie.

It was larger than he remembered. Larger and more responsive. Megan moaned softly as he played with it.

James was stunned when she wrenched herself out of his arms and whirled away.

'You...you have to stop,' she said, her voice shaking.

'But why?' he snapped. 'You want it. I know you do.'

'Yes, I do,' she admitted, her face flushing. 'I'm sorry, but we...we can't do anything right now. I have my period.'

James almost swore. But just as well he hadn't: Megan was not the sort of girl one used words like that with.

'For how long?' he asked, still a little sharply. But, hell on earth, he was in agony.

'Till Friday at least,' she said.

That was five whole days away! For a few seconds James struggled with his frustration before realising that those five days would eventually pass. After which...

'Will your period definitely be finished by Saturday?'

'Saturday should be fine,' she said, and blushed prettily.

His eyes raked over her, noting that her eyes were sparkling and her nipples hard as rocks. It was going to be difficult keeping his hands off her till then.

He'd have to work out even harder in the gym this week to work off his frustrations.

'We'll fly out to Dream Island first thing Saturday morning,' he pronounced firmly.

Megan's eyes widened. 'But you haven't even booked yet. How do you know you'll get a booking for next Saturday? Or even a flight?'

'Don't you worry your pretty little head about that. I'll organise everything. Come Saturday, we'll be on Dream Island.'

'How long will we be gone for?' she asked.

James was about to say a week. He really couldn't afford to be away from the office for longer than that at the moment. He'd just started up a new addition to his business: a casting agency to cater for the increasing number of movies being made in Australia. But then he remembered that he wasn't just whisking Megan away to have a twenty-four-seven sex-fest with her. He wanted to get her pregnant.

He'd forgotten that for a moment!

He quickly worked out the dates from what she'd told him about her period. Her peak time for conceiving would be a fortnight from today, give or take a few days either way. If they didn't leave Sydney till Saturday he'd have to extend their holiday to at least ten days, just to be on the safe side. He couldn't rely on getting her pregnant after they came back. She might go back into her shell when she returned. No, he would have to strike whilst his wife was hot. Which she was—very hot.

'I thought ten days,' he said.

She suddenly began to look worried again, for some reason.

Despite his earlier resolve to keep his hands off, he swiftly gathered her back into his arms, and kissed her again. It was worth the pain to feel her melt against him once more. Still, it was going to be a long week, sleeping beside her in bed and not being able to touch her. Knowing him, he was sure to try something and spoil everything. Better to keep her at arm's length.

A sudden idea occurred to him.

'Remember how great our wedding night was?' he said, and she nodded, her eyes glistening a little. 'Why don't we try to re-create that?'

'But…but…how?'

'If you remember, we hadn't seen each other for a few weeks before our wedding day. That time apart made our getting together again extra-special. I know it'll only be a few days this time, but we could do something similar. You could sleep down here till we go. And have your meals down here. If you promise to eat, that is. What do you think?'

'I think it's a very romantic idea,' she said, but with reservation, he thought.

'I *can* be romantic, you know,' he said teasingly.

'Can you?'

'Not often, I admit. But I can try.'

'Won't Roberta think it a bit strange if I don't come up to the house for meals?'

'I'll explain what we're doing.'

She blinked, then nodded. James smiled. That was another thing he really liked about Megan. She didn't argue with him.

'Great. Look, I'd better hotfoot it into the office and see to that booking post-haste. Don't forget to eat some of this food. I'll pick something up at work. Bye, darling.' He squeezed her shoulder as he gave her a peck on the cheek. 'See you tonight.'

'No, you won't.'

'You're right. I won't. Damn. Still, it's not that long till Saturday.' Just a bloody eternity!

'What happens if you can't get a booking?'

'I'll get a booking,' he said with a scowl. 'Even if I have to buy the whole damned island!'

CHAPTER FIVE

WHICH he would, Megan accepted ruefully as she watched him hurry out of the pool house. James Logan was not a man to fail in anything he did. He was a man amongst men. A winner.

Megan knew more about her husband than he might realise she did. When he'd left her home alone during the six weeks between their engagement and wedding, she'd spent many hours checking him out on the internet, feeding her insatiable curiosity about the powerful man she'd fallen madly in love with and was about to marry. She'd read every item of news which related to him; every single article written about his background, his professional and his private lives.

There was one heck of a lot.

Although she already knew that James's father was transport magnate Wayne Logan, Megan hadn't known that Logan senior was a self-made billionaire who'd begun life as a lowly truck driver, becoming a multimillionaire by the time he was thirty. Of course, his marriage to the daughter of his wealthy boss had given him a leg up on the ladder of success, a strategy Megan was familiar with. Megan suspected her own mother had married for money, not for love. She was sometimes ashamed of the way her extremely materialistic mother did nothing but spend her poor father's money.

At least Wayne Logan had pulled his weight, proving himself an astute businessman by building up his ailing father-in-law's trucking company into the biggest in Australia. After his father-in-law passed away, Logan had gone on to bigger and better things, expanding his transport empire overseas, buying container ships and a couple of airlines, as well as more trucks.

Logan's marriage had produced two sons. Jonathon, the elder by five years, had been killed in a car accident a few weeks after his twenty-third birthday. The Porsche he was driving—he'd run off the road and hit a telegraph pole—had been a birthday present from his doting father.

James didn't figure largely in any articles about the Logan family until he was twenty-five, at which point he'd burst into the media spotlight—not because he'd followed into the family business as his older brother had, but as the highly successful manager of several singers and actors whose previous manager had been arrested for embezzlement three years earlier. Facing financial ruin, they'd all clubbed together at that time and turned to James for help. James had set up shop as a civil litigation lawyer after leaving university, raking up business by dropping pamphlets through letter boxes.

It came out later than none of them had known James had only been twenty-two at the time. James had always looked older than he was.

But help them he had. Not by suing the man who'd fleeced them—an impossible course of action after the gambling-addicted fool had committed suicide—but by talking them into taking him on as their manager. James had always had the gift of the gab, it seemed, and a passion for the entertainment business.

It was history now that under the original contract they'd signed with him James had taken no commission for the first year, provided they did what he said, no questions asked. With little to lose—all of them were in danger of fast becoming 'has-beens' and 'never-wases'—they'd all agreed to his terms.

Within three years, every one of James Logan's clients was a success story and James was raking it in. His new company, Images, quickly became the most famous management agency in Australia, and he was dubbed 'The Makeover Man'.

That was his basic modus operandi. James made people over; gave them what he called the right image, transforming the bland and the boring into the bold and the beautiful, giving each singer and actor not just a new look but also sometimes a new name, and always a new confidence. This, combined with lots of exposure on television—in everything from telethons to reality shows to guest spots on the proliferation of breakfast programmes—made his clients some of the most well-known faces in Australia and subsequently some of the most sought-after performers.

His biggest success story back then had been Jessica Mason, a country-and-western performer in her late twenties, who'd once won a 'Golden Guitar' in her late teens, but had languished in mediocrity ever since. She'd also gained about twenty kilos in that time. James didn't change her name, though he shortened her first name to Jessie and left off the last. He personally supervised her diet and exercise programme till she was back to her optimum weight of fifty-two kilos, allowing her very good figure to emerge once more. Her long mass of rather ratty blonde hair was dyed jet-black and her wardrobe was changed from fringed suede vests and cowboy boots to long, flowing skirts, low-cut tops and jewel-encrusted sandals.

Her first album—titled 'Barefoot Gypsy'—had one of the sexiest covers ever produced, with Jessie standing next to a camp fire in a flamenco-style pose, with her skirt lifted high to expose a lot of hip and thigh, her head thrown back so that her wild black curls flowed down her back and her obviously braless breasts thrust up high against the gauzy white blouse she was almost wearing.

The album had gone gold within days; platinum within weeks. Years later it was still selling. Of course, this wasn't entirely due to the provocative cover, though it played a big part. The songs on the CD backed up the promise of the packaging, being moody and sexy, with great lyrics and throbbing rhythms.

'You still have to deliver,' James was quoted as saying when he was accused of selling sex. 'My singers can sing, and my actors can act. The trouble with the entertainment industry is that the truly talented don't always get the opportunity to show what they can do. I give my people that opportunity by promoting them in a way which gets them noticed.'

It was inevitable that James would eventually extend his business interests into the advertising industry.

'Products aren't much different from people,' he was also quoted as saying in another article after he'd started up Images Advertising. 'They require an image to be successful, as do companies. Come to me and I'll guarantee to increase your sales in six months, or I'll give you your money back.'

This extremely bold statement had seen stressed sales and marketing managers flocking to James to perform his magic. And perform it he had, with the help of the highly creative, lateral-thinking staff he'd hired.

By the age of thirty James had become a multimillionaire and something of a playboy. The internet threw up hundreds of photographs of him doing what playboys did during their leisure hours: there were snapshots of him at the races, at movie premieres, at swish charity dos and golfing tournaments; on yachts, driving sports cars and relaxing in five-star resorts.

Most of the photographs showed James with a different dolly-bird on his arm. It came as a surprise to the Press when, at the age of thirty-two, he married Jackie Foster, the

Australian supermodel. He'd been tabbed to stay a swinging bachelor for a few more years.

Megan had only felt minor jealousy over James's earlier girlfriends. They were way in the past, after all. But she'd taken one look at the photographs of James's first wedding day and realised she had a long way to go before her bridal snaps would even compare. Jackie Foster had made a simply stunning bride.

Megan still wasn't jealous. James had done a good job of convincing Megan she was what he wanted, not Jackie Foster. Suddenly, however, she'd not been happy with the way she looked. The least she could do was make the best of herself. So she'd turned to a fashion guru for help—not her overly critical mother!—and been very pleased with the result. She'd swanned down that aisle on her own wedding day believing she was truly beautiful, and also believing that she had her husband-to-be's true love.

'What a fool I was,' she muttered as she picked up a piece of toast and gave it a savage bite.

What *hadn't* she believed back then?

Thinking about her husband's lies and deceptions stirred up a hornets' nest of anger inside Megan. Some directed at James, but most directed at herself. She should have confronted him with the truth at the hospital, when the hurt had been fresh in her mind, and in her heart. She should not have left it.

It was too late now. She was trapped, not just by her unrequited love for the man, but also by her renewed desire for him. She wanted to go on that second honeymoon with him quite desperately. Wanted him to make love to her for days on end. No use pretending differently. No use thinking she was going to do or say anything which would stop that from happening.

Standing up, Megan walked over to the easel and lifted the dust cloth from the painting. What she saw there still had the power to shock her…but also to excite her.

The phone ringing startled Megan. Impossible for James to be in his office yet. He'd only left ten minutes earlier. Of course, he *could* be ringing her from his car phone, but she didn't think so. He didn't do that too often.

Megan winced at the thought it might be her mother, wanting to know the ins and outs of Hugh's wedding. She'd rung last night as Megan had been undressing for bed. Megan had put her off at the time, saying she had a headache.

Putting her mother off, however, was only ever a band-aid solution. That woman had the hide of an elephant and the tenacity of a column of ants!

When the ringing continued, an already frustrated Megan spun round and marched over to where the phone sat on a small table next to the red leather sofa. Steeling herself, she snatched it up from its cradle before slumping down onto the sofa at the same time.

'Hello,' she said, her tone not happy.

'Oh,' came a woman's voice down the line. 'Sorry. Have I caught you at a bad time?'

Not her mother, Megan realised with a mixture of relief and embarrassment. It was Nicole, Russell McClain's wife.

Nicole was the closest Megan had ever come to having a proper girlfriend. Amazingly, they'd both attended the same boarding school as teenagers but they hadn't been friends back then. Nicole had been in the class ahead of her and their paths had rarely crossed. Not that this would have made much difference. Megan hadn't been popular with girls even in her own class, possibly because she was shy, but more probably because she wasn't interested in what her classmates were interested in: clothes, make-up, internet chatrooms, mobile phones. Megan had found them all time-wasters. She'd preferred her own company to the silly chatter of her peers. She much preferred to paint, and to dream.

She *had* been interested in boys, but in a daydreaming, highly romanticised fashion. She'd thought about the opposite sex—and sex itself—quite a bit, forming a picture in her mind of what her Prince Charming would be like. Nothing like the crude, rude individuals who had gone to the all-boys school not far from her all-girls school, and whom she and her fellow pupils were forced to socialise with every once in a while. Her Mr Right had always been older, much more suave, and a very accomplished lover.

At art school, Megan had actually made a couple of male friends. But they'd both been gay. Prince Charming was nowhere in sight and, once again, her fellow female students hadn't seemed to want to know her.

By the time she'd met and married James, Megan had become used to being a loner. Suddenly being thrust into the social spotlight as James's wife had been a daunting experience to begin with. She hadn't been used to going out into the public arena. She certainly hadn't been used to hosting dinner parties, or doing the kind of thing James had probably assumed she could do. Her mother was, after all, an accomplished society matron who'd organised her daughter's wedding in six short weeks without a hitch.

Megan had coped surprisingly well, thanks to Nicole, who soon became more than just the wife of one of James's closest friends, but a personal friend as well. Megan liked her enormously. She was a terrific girl, not vain despite her incredible blonde beauty. And in no way superficial or selfish, as some rich men's wives could be.

With Nicole at her side most of the time, Megan had overcome her introverted nature to become not a social animal like James, but at least not a nervous wreck when faced with the company of the rich and famous.

After her miscarriage, however, a devastated and depressed Megan had refused to socialise at all. She'd even shunned Nicole, not able to get over the feeling that Russell must have confided the humiliating truth to his wife. She'd imagined Nicole not laughing at her, but pitying her.

Facing Nicole at Hugh's wedding had been awkward, with Megan feeling guilty over her treatment of the girl. She'd been half expecting Nicole to snub her. But Nicole had been her usual nice self, saying she was so glad to see Megan was feeling—and looking—so much better, and that they should get together some time for lunch.

Which was probably the reason for this call.

'Sorry I snapped at you,' Megan said. 'I thought you were my mother.'

Nicole laughed. 'You don't have to apologise. I have one of those, too.'

Megan had to smile. 'You do, don't you?'

'Oh, yes. She still rings me constantly and still tries to interfere, the way mothers do.'

'But you don't let her,' Megan said, recalling how Nicole had stood up to her mother at her wedding and told her to get lost.

Megan sometimes wished she could say the same to her own mother, who was not only critical but also controlling. She made Megan's father's life a misery. It was because of her mother, Megan believed, that she'd grown up lacking in confidence. Nothing was ever good enough for her mother. Perhaps if she'd had older brothers and sisters Megan would have been allowed to blossom as an individual, without being constantly pressured by her mother into becoming a 'success'.

Only one thing Megan had ever done had satisfied her mother and that was marrying James Logan. She'd actually been praised for falling pregnant so quickly; told with great pride that she was a clever, clever girl.

Janet Donnelly hadn't been shattered by her daughter's miscarriage, saying blithely that she shouldn't worry; she was already Mrs James Logan and there would be another baby in time.

Megan grimaced when she thought of her mother's reaction if she ever found the courage to leave James.

'Mum's actually not too bad these days,' Nicole said. 'Of course, it does help that she's on the other side of the world. And that I'm married to a super-rich man.'

'Mothers do seem to like that, don't they?' Megan said ruefully.

'I wouldn't worry too much about what your mother likes and doesn't like, Megan. My mum thinks I'm crazy to be working, especially when I give all my salary to charity. But what the heck? It makes me feel good. There comes a time when you have to do whatever is right for you, whatever makes *you* happy.'

Happy!

Megan knew that nothing she did was going to make her genuinely happy. She had to admit, however, that she was looking forward to next Saturday. Perverse it might be to feel hopelessly excited over going on a second honeymoon with a man who didn't love you, and who was probably only taking you away to get you pregnant. But life was perverse, she'd discovered, and so was sexual attraction. She'd tried to fight wanting James and had lost the battle.

'James is going to take me on a second honeymoon,' Megan said. There didn't seem any point in keeping it a secret, since she was determined to go.

'That's wonderful news! I'm so glad for you. When are you going?'

'Next Saturday.' She didn't add *if* James could get a booking, because she knew he would.

'That's great, Megan. Truly great.'

'James wants to try for another baby.'

'Yes, I imagine that he would. I mean…he's not getting any younger, Megan. And Russell said he's dead set on having children.'

'Yes, I know.' So dead set that he was prepared to get any old girl pregnant and marry her.

No, not any old girl. A silly, young, naïve girl who

wouldn't think to question his motives; who'd be so bowled over at such a brilliant man pursuing her that she could hardly think at all.

This time, the hornets' nest of anger was all for James.

'Look, why don't we get together for lunch one day this week?' Nicole suggested. 'We can go clothes shopping as well. You might like to buy some new things to take on your holiday.'

'Aah,' Megan said, wincing with embarrassment. 'I suppose you noticed I was wearing my going-away outfit yesterday. The thing is, Nicole, I haven't been clothes shopping for quite a while. I just haven't been interested.'

'That's understandable. You've been through a rough time, Megan. But so has James. Look, I'm sure his suggesting a second honeymoon is not just to try for another baby. He probably wants to get you away so that you can be together. He loves you a great deal, you know.'

'Actually no, I don't know that,' Megan muttered before she could think better of it.

'What? You think James doesn't love you? Why, that's ridiculous, Megan! He *adores* you.'

Megan wished she hadn't said anything now. It had been very silly of her. Still, it was good to find out that Nicole didn't seem to know the truth about her marriage. She could go to lunch with her now and not feel uncomfortable.

'Yes, I'm sure you're right,' she said hurriedly. 'I've been having this crisis of confidence since the miscarriage. Depression can do terrible things to you, Nicole. You begin to imagine all sorts of things.'

'Well, don't go imagining that James doesn't love you, my girl. Why, I remember talking to Kara one night not long after your wedding. You remember Kara, don't you? She was my best friend at school. Anyway, we both said how romantic it was that James chose to marry you. After all, rich men don't have to marry their girlfriends just because they're pregnant.

He could have bullied you into a termination, or just paid you off. Or set you up as his mistress with a child in tow. Instead, he whisked you to the altar. That's true love, if ever I saw it.'

'I'm sure you're right,' Megan said.

'I know I'm right. But I can see what you mean about you having a crisis of self-confidence. This will never do, Megan. Look, as much as James was no doubt initially attracted to your sweet self, it doesn't do to be too meek and mild. A man like James will just walk all over you in the end. There comes a time when a girl has to make her man stand up and take notice. Going on a second honeymoon is just the right time for you to sport a new image.'

Megan rather liked the sound of that. 'What kind of new image?'

'The kind James usually gives to his clients. Sexier. Bolder.'

'That sounds wonderful, Nicole. But I've never been bold, or sexy.'

'Which is why it's called a *new* image. Now, I don't want to hear any more objections. It's clear you need a push in the right direction and I'm just the girl to give you that. When did you say you were going on this honeymoon?'

'Saturday,' Megan said, feeling slightly bulldozed. But not unhappy.

'Saturday. Right. In that case I'll also make an appointment for you at this fabulous beauty salon I know. Kara took me there on my wedding day. They do the works, not just hair. It costs a bomb but what the heck? James can afford it.'

'I don't care what it costs,' Megan was astonished to hear herself saying with an upsurge of adrenaline, 'if I end up looking anything like you do.' And if she could have James look at her with genuine hunger, the kind which couldn't possibly be pretend.

* * *

By the time she hung up the phone, Nicole felt quite excited about her plans for the week. She would take Megan out to lunch tomorrow. Then clothes shopping on Wednesday and Thursday. She suspected she would need more than one day to talk Megan into the kind of wardrobe she had in mind. It would be off to the spa to spend the day on Friday. It would mean taking the week off work but that was fine. She was married to the boss.

'Russell?' she called out as she raced downstairs. 'Russell, where are you?'

No reply. He wasn't in any of the living rooms, or the kitchen. 'Russell?' she called out again, louder this time.

'I'm out here,' he replied, his voice coming from the direction of the back garden.

Nicole sometimes wished they were still living in Russell's unit at McMahon's Point. It had been a cosy little place where you always knew where the other was. But of course they needed a bigger place now.

She burst out onto the back verandah and finally found Russell, standing in the middle of the large back garden, his hands on his hips. 'What say we put a sandpit over there,' he suggested, pointing at one corner, 'and a Wendy house over there?'

'There's no hurry,' she said, but with a smile in her voice. 'The baby's not due for another six months.'

'Aah, but I only have one full day off a week, you know.'

Which was today. Monday.

Nicole pursed her lips. 'I should have known you'd revert to your workaholic ways, once I married you.'

'That's the pot calling the kettle black, madam.'

'True,' Nicole agreed. She'd really found her forte, working with Russell in his real-estate business. It gave her a buzz, finding the right house for people. She also got a buzz from being able to send her own money over to Julie, who was in the process of opening a second orphanage in Bangkok.

'So how did the call to Megan go?' Russell asked. 'I'll bet you still didn't talk her into going to lunch with you.'

'Then you'd be wrong,' she told him smugly. 'We're going tomorrow. Then I'm taking her clothes shopping on Wednesday and Thursday. And then we're off to Stephano's Beauty Spa all of Friday. Can you guess why?'

Russell spun round to stare at his wife. 'Don't tell me. She's agreed to go on a second honeymoon with James.'

'Right in one. To Dream Island, no less.'

'Fan-bloody-tastic! I've been really worried about that pair since they lost the baby.'

'I've been more worried about Megan,' Nicole said. 'She's a vulnerable sort of girl, isn't she? Did you know she's been entertaining this crazy idea that James might not love her?'

'What?'

'Yes, I was just as shocked as you. I mean, we both know he does. Now, why are you giving me that funny look? What is it that you know that I don't know?' Nicole was crossing her arms in exasperation when the penny dropped. 'Oh, no!' she exclaimed, her arms dropping to her sides in shock. 'He doesn't love her, does he? He just married her for the child. That's why he was so devastated when she miscarried.'

'Afraid so,' Russell admitted with a sigh.

'The creep!'

'Don't be too hard on him, Nicole. He wants a family, and Jackie refused to give him one. What was he supposed to do? Ride off alone into the sunset? That's not James's way. He's a survivor and a doer.'

Nicole's eyes narrowed. 'Did he get Megan pregnant on purpose before he married her?'

'I think so. Not that he told me so directly. James doesn't talk about his personal life much. I do know, however, that he's still hung up on Jackie.'

'That self-centred cow? Megan makes ten of her!'

'We both know that.'

'Poor Megan... No wonder she's lost confidence in herself. She probably *feels* the fact that he's not in love with her. Thank goodness I managed to convince her that she was just imagining things.'

'That's good. Very good. Look, who knows? He might fall in love with her in time.'

'Hmm. That's unlikely to happen unless she changes,' Nicole said thoughtfully. 'She's got to stop being Megan the mouse. My makeover this week will be none too soon.'

'Don't do anything too dramatic, Nicole. James likes Megan the way she is.'

'Yes, but he's not in love with Megan the way she is. She has to come out of her shell a bit. Shake him up. Be bolder, and sexier.'

'That's mission impossible, Nicole.'

'Don't be silly. It's just a matter of window dressing. Men are visual creatures. If she looks sexier, he'll see her as sexier and treat her differently. Then she'll *feel* sexier and act sexier, and things will snowball from there.'

'If you say so.'

'I do say so.'

Russell shrugged. 'I presume you didn't tell her about our baby.'

'Lord, no. That would only have made her miserable. You haven't told James yet, have you?'

'No.'

'Then don't. At least not till they get back from this holiday, which hopefully will be a success.'

'If I know James it will be.'

'He's not God, you know,' Nicole said somewhat irritably. James had never been her favourite amongst Russell's male friends. Even less so now!

'Don't tell James that. Or his clients.'

'The trouble with James Logan,' Nicole went on waspishly,

'is that he's way too intelligent and way too good-looking for his own good.'

'He does have a big ego,' Russell conceded.

'And a big something else, I'll bet.'

'Nicole McClain!' her husband exclaimed with mock-outrage.

'Oh, don't give me any of that! You and I both know your friend's reputation with women. Before he married Jackie Foster he had a string of playthings a mile long.'

'That was years ago. He's changed.'

'Oh, phooey. He hasn't changed. Not deep down. He's a bad boy in the bedroom and don't you dare try to tell me differently.'

'I seem to recall you were partial to my being a bad boy in the bedroom when we first met,' Russell said.

'That was different,' Nicole said with a hoity toss of her long blonde hair.

'How was it different?'

'We were in love.'

'Megan's in love with James.'

'Yes, but James is not in love with *her*!'

'What she doesn't know doesn't hurt her.'

'That's so typical of a man!' Nicole exclaimed, stamping her foot at the same time. 'They can never see beyond the moment.'

'That's not true,' Russell defended. 'I'm sure James would rather things be different. But they're not. Like I said earlier, we can't always choose who we fall in love with. You should know that better than anyone, Nicole. Have some empathy for James, for pity's sake. You have plenty of empathy for other people.'

Nicole was taken aback by Russell's stance. It was rare for him to criticise her. But once she thought about his very wise words, she saw that she had been judgemental of James. The trouble was she couldn't always look at a rich man with unbiased eyes.

'You're right,' she said. 'I haven't been fair to James. I just wish he hadn't married a girl like Megan. She's just so…fragile.'

'With a mother like that? I suspect that underneath Megan's fragile exterior lurks a spine of steel.'

'Maybe…'

'Definitely! Now, no more talk about James and Megan. And no more worrying about them. They're adults. They'll work it out.'

CHAPTER SIX

SATURDAY morning found Megan with another crisis of confidence, this time of her own making. Whatever had possessed her to listen to Nicole's advice? It wasn't the new clothes which bothered her so much—though they were somewhat in-your-face—but what she'd been talked into doing at the beauty salon yesterday.

She must have been mad!

The phone ringing brought a groan. It would be James, wanting to know if she was ready. He'd phoned late last night, saying that he would pick her up at eight on the dot this morning, which was less than five minutes away.

Megan had been up since her alarm clock had gone off shortly after six, getting herself ready. She'd declined Roberta's offer of a breakfast tray, saying she'd get something to eat at the airport. She'd known her stomach would be churning with nervous tension and unable to digest any food.

And now the moment was here, the moment she'd been dreaming about all week and which she was suddenly dreading.

'Yes, James,' she said on picking up the phone. 'I'm ready.' As ready as she would ever be!

'I'll be down shortly.'

Megan hung up then hurried over to inspect herself in the long wall mirror for the umpteenth time that morning, turning this way and that so that she could see herself from all angles.

It was just as well that the white hipster trousers were made of stretch material, she decided, because they were extremely tight, hugging her *derrière* and thighs like a second skin. When combined with the rather glitzy silver high-heeled sandals she was wearing, they made her legs look very long. And sexy.

The whole outfit was sexy, especially the black and white top, which had an extremely low-cut neckline. Perhaps if she'd gone braless it might have looked less provocative. But the lacy black push-up bra Nicole had chosen to go with it created an eye-popping cleavage. It seemed her recent weight loss hadn't produced much loss there.

Megan was rather relieved that she had a denim jacket to go over everything. Though it wouldn't hide the cleavage part. Besides, the jacket would have to come off once she got on the plane. Or, at the very latest, when they disembarked in Cairns. Their destination had an average temperature of twenty-eight degrees, even at this time of the year, along with high humidity.

Her holiday wardrobe catered for the heat, consisting of several skimpy tops and shorts, a few skimpy sundresses, and two very skimpy swimming costumes: a red bikini, which had an outrageous bottom half—it was just a thong—and a colourful one-piece which had looked deceptively modest on the rack, but wasn't really.

Despite having the figure to wear such clothes now, Megan still didn't feel comfortable with flaunting her body. She'd been talked into most of her purchases by Nicole, who was extremely persuasive. No wonder that girl was doing well in real estate.

I do look good, Megan decided. That beauty salon really knew its stuff. It was just that the girl gazing back at her in the mirror didn't quite look like her. That girl was way too fashionable, and funky. And yes, sexy.

There was that word again. Sexy.

Suddenly she thought of the painting which she'd finished last night and which was hidden away in the cupboard, along with the other one. Both were good. Very good. Her best work.

Would she ever dare show either of them to James?

Megan doubted it very much.

At last, James thought as he hurried towards the pool-room door.

In a few hours, they would be in Cairns. Then, after a short helicopter flight, on Dream Island, where they'd be alone in the exclusive resort's most luxurious—and most expensive—private villa.

He could hardly wait!

This past week had been one of the longest weeks in his life. He'd managed to distract himself somewhat from his ongoing frustration by working long hours in the office, after which he'd worked out in the gym till he was tired enough to sleep. But the time had still dragged. It might have helped if he'd been able to play golf at some stage. Golf always distracted and relaxed him. But Hugh was away on his honeymoon and Russell was snowed under with making more millions selling houses, courtesy of Nicole spending most of the week with Megan.

James wasn't into playing golf by himself.

He'd woken this morning feeling both excited and relieved. Now he just felt excited.

He didn't bother to knock. He just barged right in. At which point he stopped dead in his tracks.

'My God!' he exclaimed.

* * *

If nothing else, following Nicole's advice had been worth this moment, Megan thought with a wild rush of pleasure.

The look in James's eyes might not be love, but it was the next best thing. His gaze fairly sizzled as it raked over her from top to toe, his mouth remaining open with shock.

Finally it snapped shut, and he smiled. It was a super-sexy smile.

'Wow!' he said.

That one word went a long way to restoring the confidence she'd once felt around the man she loved.

Megan returned his smile. 'Nicole said it was time for Megan the mouse to be dispensed with.'

James looked taken aback. 'What an awful thing for her to say!'

'Not at all. I agreed with her completely. It was time for a change. So what do you think of the new me?' She twirled in a complete circle, her newly layered and much brighter hair swishing back and forth across her shoulders.

'I think,' he said, his dark eyes glittering, 'that if we don't get out of here right now, we might miss that plane. So point me to your luggage, O gorgeous one, and let's go!'

An elated Megan did just that before sweeping up her fitted denim jacket and her new pewter holdall, popping on her new designer sunglasses then heading for the door.

James kept staring at her all the way to the airport, his expression ranging from a wry amusement to open admiration. He didn't seem quite as amused during their walk through the terminal, however, when other men started staring at her as well. One even whistled as she walked past.

'Lecherous bastard,' James muttered under his breath.

Megan wasn't sure if she liked the attention or not. It felt strange. She wasn't used to being ogled. But she liked her husband's jealousy. Still, she was glad when they were finally settled on board and it was just him and her together, in the business-class section of the plane.

Flaunting her breasts in public wasn't really her style.

But I might get used to it, came the unexpected thought.

'I can see,' James said after they'd stowed their things and snapped on their seat belts, 'that I'll have to polish up my black belt in karate.'

'What? What for?'

'To fight off all the other guys.'

Megan blushed with pleasure. 'Don't be silly.'

'I'm not. Honest to goodness, Megan. I hardly recognised you this morning. You look so sexy it's sinful.'

Megan decided not to take offence. Because he was right: she did look different and, yes, *sexy*.

'I was at the beauty salon all day yesterday,' she told him, 'so I should warn you before the credit-card bill comes in that looking like this costs a small fortune.' For which exorbitant price, however, they'd given her the works. Her teeth had been whitened, her long brown hair cut, styled and colour-enhanced, her eyebrows plucked, her lips plumped, all her nails painted. She'd been waxed, buffed and polished, till every inch of her skin was as silky-smooth as a surfboard. *Every inch.*

Oh, dear… She'd forgotten about that for a moment. Megan swallowed nervously. Should she mention it now, or leave it for all to be revealed later?

In the end, she stayed silent on the subject. There was nothing to be gained by saying anything prematurely. What was done was done.

'My wardrobe cost a bomb as well,' she confessed instead, using one of Nicole's pet phrases. It did seem, however, that the kind of beauty which turned men's heads cost one heck of a lot of money.

But there was only one man whose head she wanted to turn.

'My money is your money, darling,' that man said smilingly, and leant over to pick up her right hand.

* * *

James knew immediately that he shouldn't have touched her. Not here, not now. But it was too late...

He watched her with a mixture of curiosity and arousal as he ran his tongue lightly over the tips of her fingers, then quite deliberately drew her middle finger into his mouth.

The old Megan would have been shocked. What would this new Megan do?

He saw the surprise in her eyes slowly change to something else. Her pupils dilated, her eyelids grew heavy. When he sucked on her finger, her mouth fell open with a small gasp. Not with shock but with pleasure; sheer sensual pleasure.

James had always known Megan was a responsive and passionate creature, only her shyness—and her lack of experience—stopping him from taking their lovemaking along more adventurous lines. He hadn't wanted to upset her with demands she might find repulsive, or disgusting.

He could see, however, that this new Megan might just be ready to expand her horizons. It excited him to think of her doing to him what he was doing to her finger. Excited him to a point where he knew he would soon have to stop.

Seeing the flight attendant approaching down the aisle with a trolley of drinks forced him to take Megan's finger out of his mouth and return her hand to her arm rest. It was gratifying, however, to hear her soft moan of protest. Clearly she was as turned on as he was, maybe even more so. There was a glazed look in her eyes which suggested she'd totally surrendered herself to what he was doing, possibly even becoming unaware of her surroundings. Intense sexual arousal could do that at times.

James realised that their second honeymoon was going to be even better than he'd hoped.

'Would you and the lady like a drink, sir?' the steward asked.

James turned his head towards Megan, who was still looking dazed. 'Champagne for you, darling?'

She blinked, then nodded.

'Champagne for the lady and a double Scotch for me,' he ordered. 'No ice.'

Megan positively gulped the champagne whilst he sipped his whisky very slowly, all the while savouring deliciously erotic thoughts of what lay ahead. This new Megan didn't stand a chance, not now that he knew she was ripe and ready. Neither would their lovemaking be confined to the bedroom. His wife was going to be his in ways she hadn't been before. Making her a mother was suddenly not James's main priority. First, he aimed to fix the frustration he'd been living with for over three months now.

The steward stopped on his way back down the aisle and offered top-ups for them both.

Megan stared down at the glass in her hands, shocked to see that it was empty.

'No, not right now,' she said, and handed the steward the glass. She could already feel the effect of the alcohol on her empty stomach, her head spinning a little.

Though that might not be the champagne. She'd been light-headed ever since James had done what he'd done. Her hands gripped the arm rests at the memory of how it had felt when he'd sucked on her finger. She hadn't wanted him to stop. Hadn't given a thought to where they were, or that other people on the plane might see them.

When he'd withdrawn his finger she'd even cried out in protest.

Recalling that brought a sudden wave of embarrassment. What must James think of her?

'Don't,' he said quietly beside her.

Her head turned his way. 'Don't what?'

'Don't be embarrassed.'

'How did...?' She broke off once she realised her face must have gone red. It still felt hot. 'You must think me very silly,' she said, all her earlier elation dissolving into dismay. Nicole's project of making her over into a bolder, sexier woman had been doomed to failure from the start. She just didn't have that kind of confidence. She never had had, even before her miscarriage.

'I don't think you're silly at all,' James said. 'I admire that you've made some changes to your appearance this past week. You do look incredible. But that's not the same as changing the person you are inside. You're basically shy, Megan. You could never be an exhibitionist, for which I'm grateful. I wouldn't have married a girl who liked my making love to her in public.'

'But that's what you just did!' she protested. 'And I *did* like it. Sort of...'

His smile confused her.

'I know,' he said, 'but that's because you were so turned on you forgot you were in public.'

'How do you know that?'

'Trust me. I know.'

She just stared at him.

'I'm a lot older than you, Megan. And a lot more experienced. I recognised the signs. I'm sorry if I embarrassed you. I didn't mean to do what I did. I was just so turned on by the new you that I lost control for a moment.'

'You did?' She found the concept amazing. That her super-cool husband could ever lose control. She didn't think it was possible. Not with her, anyway. Maybe he did desire her for real. Maybe his passion wasn't pretend.

'Don't sound so surprised. Do you have any idea how frustrated I've been these past few months? Some nights I've been climbing the walls.'

Aah... So it wasn't desire for *her* so much which had made him lose control, just the desire for sex.

Megan should have realised that. For a moment dismay threatened. But she fought it off by addressing the situation with some common-sense logic. There was no use pining for the moon. She'd known the score when she came on this second honeymoon. He didn't love her and that was that. It seemed, however, that he hadn't been unfaithful to her. Be thankful for small mercies, girl. And take full advantage of his frustration.

Because, let's face it, he wasn't the only one who'd been climbing the walls this past week.

She set surprisingly steady eyes upon him. 'How many girls have you had over the years?' she asked.

'What a question! I've got no idea.'

'*That* many…'

'I wouldn't worry about any of them, if I were you. They were all banished from my mind the moment you came along.'

Well, of course they had, she thought with a degree of cynicism which surprised her. I was chosen to be the mother of your children.

'Why me?' she suddenly asked, despite knowing that she was treading on thin ice.

'Because you were perfect,' came his smoothly delivered reply.

Oh, he was good, he was very good.

Megan decided to steer the conversation on to a safer topic. 'Did you mind that I was a virgin?'

He looked startled. 'Mind? Why would I have minded?'

She shrugged. 'Because I was inexperienced. I dare say, after a while, you found me rather boring in bed.'

'I never found you boring in bed.'

'Oh, come, now, James. If we're going to start again, we should at least be honest about things in the bedroom.'

James realised the situation could get sticky here very quickly. 'Megan, darling. I am being honest. I never thought you boring in bed. At the same time, that doesn't mean that I would not have, one day, moved our love life in a more… imaginative direction. I get the impression you wouldn't object if I did that during our second honeymoon. If I have got the wrong message, however, I would suggest you say so now.'

'What do you mean by a more…imaginative direction?'

'I don't think this is the time or the place to go into detail. If you trust me, however, as the more experienced partner, I will show you when we get to Dream Island.' His eyes caressed hers in the most seductive fashion. 'I promise I won't do anything you might find too…um—er—much.'

'Such as what?'

He shrugged. 'Such as tying you to the bed,' he said rather flippantly. Then immediately wished he hadn't.

Her eyes flared wide. But he didn't spot any alarm in their depths, only surprise. And perhaps a flicker of excitement.

James put mild bondage down as a possibility. It stirred his flesh unbearably to think of Megan lying naked on a bed, her arms stretched up above her head, her wrists secured to the bed head. He suspected Megan might enjoy the experience as well. She could surrender her will to his, as she had when he'd sucked her finger just now. She would be powerless to stop him from going down on her. She would enjoy that, once he got her past her shyness. He was sure of it.

'Of course, I might,' he continued recklessly, 'but only if you ask me to…' When he held her dilated eyes with effort-less ease, he knew she was going to do everything he wanted.

The steward chose that precise moment to interrupt with their lunch. James noted Megan's furious blush as her tray was handed over to her. No doubt she was worried that the man might have overheard what they'd said. Or possibly it was the heat of arousal which was flaming her cheeks.

James hoped it was the latter. But that was probably because his own flesh was appallingly excited.

It was a pity that they were still a couple of hours from landing in Cairns, and possibly another hour before they were ensconced in total privacy on Dream Island. He really would have to stop having this kind of provocative conversation. It wouldn't do for him to be too turned on. He had no intention of rushing things with Megan.

James exercised some ruthless control over his mind—and his body—during lunch, after which he put back his seat and told Megan that he was going to have a nap.

'Wake me when we get there, darling,' he said, and closed his eyes…

CHAPTER SEVEN

DREAM ISLAND was not a large island. Neither was it very far from the mainland. But it had everything that a romantic getaway required: lots of beautiful little beaches with the whitest of white sand, a variety of restaurants staffed by some of the best chefs in the world and an array of five-star accommodation to suit every taste, from the swish hotel situated right next to the main beach to individual villas dotted around the extensive tropical gardens and totally self-contained bures positioned in the more remote parts of the island, all of which had either their own private pool, or their own private beach.

The two-bedroomed villa James had secured for their second honeymoon was the only one on the island which had both a private beach and a pool. It was outrageously expensive and was often occupied by royalty and rock stars, or so he'd been told, as well as the odd Australian billionaire who was prepared to spend anything to impress and impregnate his second wife.

Not that James was thinking about babies by the time their plane arrived in Cairns and they finally made it by helicopter over to Dream Island. He was, however, very definitely thinking about making love to Megan, his resolve to keep his mind off that subject having disappeared the moment they landed.

The extra time that it took for them to be further transported by beach buggy through a dense tropical forest to their accommodation irritated the death out of him. But any frustration was waylaid once he saw what the two-thousand-dollar-a-day price tag provided.

Not only was their Bali-style villa suitably luxurious, but it was also extremely well-equipped for the kind of erotic interludes James had begun planning on the plane. There was a massive master bedroom complete with a king-sized bed, and an opulently decked-out *en suite* bathroom which had a double shower and a sunken spa bath. The living room was equally accommodating, with a selection of large, comfy sofas, a couple of hedonistic-looking rugs and a massive plasma television set.

Add to that total privacy—security along the only road which led to their villa was visibly tight—and you had the perfect conditions for what James was thinking of.

But first he had to get rid of the eager-beaver escort who'd brought them here, and who'd been showing them around and going through his well-practised spiel for the last ten minutes.

'You only have to pick up any of the phones,' the fellow was saying, having already pointed out the extensions in the living room, bedroom, bathroom and kitchen, 'and Reception at the resort will answer immediately. Your villa will be serviced whenever and at whatever time you request. We've found that honeymooners, especially, prefer this method, rather than Housekeeping just showing up each and every morning. Your kitchen is well-stocked with food and all manner of drink, but we also deliver meals and picnic baskets on request. All food and drink on the island is included in the tariff you've already paid. There is never any extra charge for guests staying in this particular villa, even at the à la carte restaurants. Now, here is the key to your own personal beach buggy, which is parked in the carport behind the villa. Not that you'll need it to go to the beach. As you've already seen, it's less than fifty metres from your front door. You will, however, need the buggy to get back to the main resort, and the restaurants. Let's see, now, I think that's all. Do you have any further questions?' he finished up with a cheesy smile.

'I'm sure you've covered everything,' James returned as he pocketed the key, after which he extracted a fifty-dollar note from his wallet. 'Thanks,' he said as he handed the money over.

'Thank *you*, sir. This is most appreciated.'

'And so is your departure,' James muttered under his breath as the young man hurried off.

At last he was alone with Megan, who'd disappeared somewhere, James realised on glancing around, probably into the master bedroom. He immediately strode off in that direction. Yes, there she was, standing in the middle of the room, staring at the bed.

James's eyes, however, went to the bed head.

It was made of cherry-coloured cane, like the rest of the furniture. There were no bedposts, but the cane in the head-board wasn't all that tightly woven. There were plenty of places to wind a scarf through, or a man's tie. Not that he'd brought any ties with him.

'So what do you think of the place?' James asked, realising, suddenly, that Megan hadn't said a single word since they'd arrived. Not that she'd had much chance, with that chap chattering fifty to the dozen from the moment he picked them up at the heliport.

Megan scooped in a deep breath and let it out slowly, trying with all her might to rediscover the confidence James had imbued in her this morning. But it was no use. The new bolder, sexier Megan was definitely in danger of reverting to being Megan the mouse, this depressing process having started the moment James settled back in his seat on that plane and closed his eyes.

At first she'd been stunned by his ability to relax when he should have been as cripplingly turned on as she was. Then, once it looked as if he'd actually gone to sleep, she'd just wanted to cry.

In the end, she'd put her own seat back too and tried to blank her mind. But there had been no peace for her, just the most undermining thoughts. Clearly, she had a long way to go before she became the kind of woman to seriously excite her man-of-the-world husband. Once James had got over his surprise at her new 'image', he'd seemed more amused than aroused, a suspicion confirmed when he'd gone to sleep.

By the time the plane had landed in Cairns and they made the quick transfer to Dream Island, she wished she'd never agreed to come.

Somehow she found a smile as she turned to face her husband. 'It must have cost you a small fortune.'

'It surely did. But it's worth every cent. I especially love the privacy. I think I'll become a nudist for the next ten days. Care to join me?'

Megan stared at him in horror. Or was it panic?

James quickly realised that the sexy new Megan he'd picked up this morning was still a work in progress. Clearly, she *wanted* to become more sexually adventurous. Wanted to try different things. But such a radical change took a lot of courage, and a degree of confidence which would occasionally fail her, such as now.

James knew he came across as a highly confident person, but there had been times during his younger years when he hadn't always been so sure of himself and his abilities. He could still remember what it was like to be afraid of failure— hell, he'd gone right out on a limb when he'd first started Images—so he could empathise with what Megan was feeling and what she was trying to do.

But he wasn't about to let her go back into her shell.

Still, he might have to take things a little slower than he'd planned on the plane, and not expect too much too soon.

'But first things first,' he went on. 'Are you hungry? There's loads of stuff in that kitchen.'

'No, thanks,' she replied, still looking uncomfortable. 'I had enough to eat on the plane. But I think I might go and have a shower. It's a lot hotter up here than I thought it would be at this time of the year.'

'You're right, it is. That sounds like a good idea. I'll have one with you.'

Megan's eyes flew wide, confirming what James had been thinking; that now the moment was at hand, she was suffering from a crisis in confidence.

The sudden vulnerability in her face touched him. He'd always found her air of innocence enchanting. But the time for innocence had passed now. She'd shown him today that they could share more than sweet sex, and he wanted that. He wanted it badly.

James knew he wouldn't be doing her any favours by letting her revert to her former shy self.

'You'll like it,' he said with a warmly encouraging smile as he walked over to her. 'Trust me.'

CHAPTER EIGHT

TRUST him!

Megan could not have imagined two more ironic words.

But it wasn't trust which was the issue at this moment. It was embarrassment. Megan's face flamed some more as she pictured herself standing before James, not just nude, but totally denuded.

James was taken aback by this second blush, which was fiercer than the first. He didn't try to second-guess her this time, deciding that the time for talking was over. It was time for action!

Megan welcomed his pulling her into his arms and kissing her, welcomed his taking charge. It was what he was good at, after all. Being the boss. He'd been extremely masterful with her when they'd first met, sweeping her off her feet so quickly she'd had little time to worry or wonder what lay behind his claim at being overcome by her charms. That was what she wished for now. To blindly wallow in his seeming passion for her. That was why she'd come here with him after all. To experience his expert lovemaking once more.

Megan wasn't under any illusion that their marriage would really last. How could it when she didn't want to have another baby?

She shouldn't have been feeling guilty over that. He was the only who should be feeling guilty. But James and guil simply did not co-exist. He was a ruthless, cold-blooded devil!

No, not totally cold-blooded, she conceded with a groan as his arms tightened around her, bringing her already dangerously heated body in closer contact with his. The evidence of *his* arousal, jabbing with all its flagrant and flattering urgency into her stomach, banished any guilt, her own desire for him taking over once more. Her arms tightened around his neck, the action pressing her breasts flat against the hard wall of his chest.

Somehow he swept her up off the floor without lifting his lips from hers, the kiss continuing as he strode from the bedroom into the bathroom. He didn't stop kissing her till he lowered her back onto her by then slightly unsteady feet and started lifting her top up over her head.

'Much as I love this delicious black bra on you,' he said as he tossed her black and white top carelessly aside, 'it has to go.'

Although he went straight to the hidden front clasp, he took his time undoing it, holding her eyes with his as he did. It seemed ages before the two cups parted company, Megan's heartbeat racing by the time her breasts were finally bared.

Only then did his eyes drop to them.

'Even more delicious,' he said thickly.

Megan sucked in some much needed air in anticipation of his touching her startlingly erect nipples. But he didn't. Instead, his hands went to the waistband of her white jeans.

Now her pulse went wild. Soon, he would see what she had done. Would he be surprised? Shocked? Pleased? Did he like that kind of thing? Nicole had inferred most men did.

She hoped James did. She could not bear to see disgust in his eyes when he looked at her.

'James,' she suddenly blurted out.

He lifted somewhat frustrated eyes to her face. 'What?'

'I…I have to tell you something.'

'Nothing bad, I hope.'

'Not really bad…'

'That still sounds ominous.'

Megan wished she hadn't said anything now. It was proving more awkward to confess than to just let him see for himself.

But it was too late now.

'Yesterday,' she said, swallowing, 'when I went to the beauty salon, I…um…I had a wax job.'

His frown showed confusion. 'And?'

'All over,' she choked out.

His eyebrows arched. But then he smiled. It was a very sexy smile. 'You naughty little minx.'

James loved it when she blushed this time, loved it that she could be both embarrassed and aroused at the same time.

Till he'd met Megan he hadn't had anything to do with virgins. He'd always preferred experienced girls.

But he was finally able to see why some men had this thing for virgins, especially ones who were ready and willing to be taught the many and varied pleasures of the flesh. Which obviously Megan now was. His head filled with endless erotic possibilities, and positions.

'Just give me half a sec, sweetheart,' he said, and fell to attacking the buttons on his shirt. 'I have a strong suspicion I should get myself naked before we go any further with you. God, but you look so sexy like that,' he went on as he stripped right off. 'I think I'll have you go round half-naked the whole time we're here. Or perhaps just wearing those shoes. My, but they're sexy shoes.'

Megan was glad he'd mentioned her shoes, giving her an excuse to look down instead of staring at what he looked like in his underpants, and then out of them. She'd forgotten how overwhelmingly male he was, naked.

'It's almost a shame for you to have to take those shoes off,' he went on, his socks whizzing past her eyes as they joined the pile of discarded clothes on the turquoise tiled floor, 'but you can always put them on later, after we get out of the shower.'

The image he created startled Megan, sending her eyes jerking back up to his. The idea of walking around naked before him, with nothing on but high heels, was too daunting for words.

'But first things first,' he said as he reached forward and unsnapped the waistband of her jeans. 'I don't know about you but I suddenly feel very hot indeed.'

His dark eyes glittered as he slid the zip right down to her crotch, exposing the white satin panties she was wearing. When he took possession of the waistband at her hips and started to push down, Megan held her breath.

But almost immediately, he stopped.

'Methinks you'll have to kick those shoes off first,' he said.

She did, scooping in a deep breath at the same time.

'And now the rest,' he ordered. 'You do it. I want to watch.'

Megan swallowed. But there was no question of not obeying him, any nerves far outweighed by her desires. It was cruel, the way he could make her want him. Cruel and ruthless.

But there was no point in fighting him. She'd reached the point of no return at some stage during this past week, and nothing short of death would stop her now.

James wasn't sure if she would do it…undress in front of him. But yes! She did!

Her obedience produced a flash of triumph, plus pride in the courage it was taking for a girl of her nature to do something she would consider bold. Brazen, even.

James's satisfaction, however, was soon forgotten as the sight before him unfolded. My God, how beautiful she was! Despite her recent weight loss, her body was perfectly pro-portioned, and deliciously curvy, with ripe, full breasts, a tiny waist and a generous curve of hip anchored by long, shapely legs.

Perhaps he should not have been so surprised. But he'd never seen her standing up in the nude before, only lying down and usually under sheets.

'You look like a Greek goddess,' he complimented as his eyes raked over her. 'No, don't cover yourself,' he warned sharply when her hands went to hide her denuded sex. 'I want to look at you there.' And touch you there. And tongue you there.

And she was going to let him. She was going to let him do whatever he wanted to do with her.

OK, so there was still a measure of shock in her eyes. But along with the shock lay excitement. Her breasts were rising and falling with her quickened heartbeat, her lips falling apart as she struggled to drag more air into her lungs. James felt supremely confident that if he touched her down there she would be wet, very wet.

Megan wished he would stop looking at her like that and just do something. *Anything.* It had been agony taking off the rest of her clothes, especially her panties. She'd never felt so naked in her life, or so shockingly turned on.

'Stay right where you are,' he commanded. 'Don't move. Don't cover yourself.'

Megan's hands curled into fists by her sides as she watched him slide back the shower screen and step inside to turn on the taps, taking his time to adjust the temperature and the twin shower heads to his satisfaction till he returned to her.

'Come,' he said, and took her hand in his.

He led her into the middle of the stall, where the streams of water met, positioning her so that the shower rained down like a tropical storm over her, front and back, plastering her hair to her head and travelling over her curves in erotic rivulets. Her gasp was one of surprise, for she'd never imagined water could be so erotic. When she closed her eyes and tipped her head back to clear her hair from her face, the hot spray beat even harder on her uplifted breasts, making her already erect nipples tighten further.

When the stream of water in her face suddenly stopped, her eyes flew open to find that James had moved in front of her and the water was now beating on his back.

James was about to reach out and pull Megan to him when he saw the look in his wife's eyes.

Never had he seen such excitement in a woman's face, or such hunger.

He yanked her back under the water, spinning her around so that he could imprison her against him with one arm whilst he readied her body for him with his free hand.

Not that she needed readying, James was soon to discover. She wasn't just wet for him, she was on fire, squirming against his hand, pushing her buttocks back up against him in the most provocative fashion. There was little question of any protracted foreplay. He had to get himself inside her, and quickly!

Whirling her back round to face him, he wound her arms up around his neck then lifted her right knee high up towards his left hip. Holding it there, he took himself in his other hand and angled himself up between her legs.

'Yes,' he bit out at the feel of her flesh swallowing his.

Her raw moan echoed his own pleasure. Pleasure *and* passion. It wasn't enough to just be inside her. The desire to move was both violent and urgent. James half carried her over to the tiled wall, which provided some support for her back so that he could pound up into her. There was no finesse in his lovemaking, just a desperate need for release from the frustration of the last few months. Not just physical frustration, but also emotional. He wanted to experience Megan's orgasm almost as much as his own. Only then would he know for sure that he had his wife back again and that they had a future together. For a while there, he'd been afraid that another of his marriages was doomed to failure.

But not any more. Megan obviously still loved him and wanted him. More than ever, he realised with a hot surge of triumph when he felt her splinter apart in his arms simultaneously with his own climax. Bracing his hands against the tiled walls, he shut his eyes tight and wallowed at length in the intensity of her contractions. They went on and on, milking him dry in the most satisfying way.

Finally they stopped, her arms dropping away from his neck. With a thoroughly sated sigh he withdrew and stepped back from her. Only then did he open his eyes, shocked to find that Megan's were flooded with tears. Alarm and concern shot through him like twin daggers.

'Megan! Darling! What's wrong?'

She couldn't seem to answer him. She just shook her head from side to side, tears streaming down her cheeks.

He cupped her shoulders gently and searched her bleak-looking face. 'Did I hurt you?'

Again, she shook her head.

'You're tired,' he said, and cuddled her to him. 'Travelling is always tiring.' Either that or she was experiencing some kind of post-climactic downer. Some women could get very emotional after having an orgasm, especially intense ones like Megan had just experienced. Not that she'd ever cried after sex before. But people did change. Megan had changed.

James could not discount that her tears might still have something to do with the baby they'd lost. But he really didn't want to go there. He'd never been a great believer in rehashing the past. What good did it do to go over and over traumatic events? It could only revive awful memories and the emotions associated with them. Losing the baby had hurt him, too. But in the end you had to make a choice. Either to wallow in your grief, or to move on.

When life proved difficult—even distressing—James had

always chosen to move on. It had pleased him earlier this week that Megan had finally made that choice as well. She'd pleased him too today with her changed attitude towards sex. She was becoming a grown-up woman at last, rather than a naïve young girl.

'Come back under the warm water,' he said when she started to shiver. 'There. That's better, isn't it? Rest your back against me and I'll get you all nice and clean.'

He hadn't meant to arouse her again with the shower gel. Hadn't thought it could happen so quickly. But the moment his soapy hand grazed over her nipples, he felt them stiffen. Felt her body stiffen all over. Incredible!

For the moment, he himself was totally spent. So he knew he wasn't capable of having intercourse again with her for a while. But he could still make love to her. Of course he could. But would she let him do what he had in mind?

He supposed there was only one way to find out.

'Just a short delay, beautiful,' he said, and switched off the taps. 'And a change of venue.'

Megan barely had time to think before she was roughly dried with one towel, wrapped up in another, then scooped up into his arms. Not that she wanted to think. Thinking only made her miserable, as it had a while ago after James had had rather rough sex with her up against the shower wall.

She'd actually thrilled to every wild, wonderful moment of it. But what had her mind done afterwards? Made her wish for the moon, that was what. Made her want what she couldn't have: not just her husband's lovemaking, but his love too.

As if that was ever going to happen! She could tart herself up as much as she liked and all she could hope for was some increased lust on his part. He'd been married to a supermodel, for pity's sake, and he hadn't loved *her*. What chance did *she* have?

So just focus on the sex, Megan, she lectured herself

sternly as he carried her back into the bedroom. You can at least enjoy that.

'Hold on to me,' he ordered her, supporting her towel-encased body with one hand whilst he swept back the tropical-printed quilt with the other.

The sheets were cream satin and cool. Or so she discovered when James lowered her onto them, then whisked the towel away. He felt cool too, she noticed, when he stretched out beside her. Cool and wet, droplets of water glistening all over his shoulders and across the dark mat of curls which covered the middle of his chest.

'This is much better,' he said as he smoothed her still damp hair back from her face. 'Much more comfortable.'

He kissed her then. Kissed her and stroked her till she was trembling. When he moved over her, she held her breath in anticipation of his entering her. But he did nothing of the kind, Megan watching, wide-eyed and lips parted, as he slid down her body, kissing her as he went. Her breasts first, then her stomach, then further down.

Oh, lord, she thought dazedly, her hands grasping great clumps of sheet by her sides.

A small part of her squirmed to think James was down there, doing what he was doing. The rest of her didn't give a damn. Not if it felt like this!

His lips and tongue were everywhere, kissing her, licking her, sucking her. His fingers were just as merciless, adding to her erotic torment with a highly intimate exploration. She could not believe the things he did. Could not believe she was enjoying his taking such outrageous liberties with her body. Could not believe it when he suddenly stopped.

Her cry was a cry of the most acute frustration.

'Trust me,' he said after he rested his head on the soft swell of her stomach.

Megan almost jackknifed from the bed when he started stroking his hand over the smooth skin of her pubic bone.

'I love the way you look now,' he murmured with a wicked smile, before lowering his head back to her by then tight-as-a-drum belly.

He was a wicked man, she decided breathlessly when he resumed what he'd been doing before. More wicked than she'd realised. The tension he was creating in her was both pleasure and pain. Agony and ecstasy. She would have done anything for him, if only he'd let her come.

But once again his head lifted before that happened.

'Amazing,' he said with an almost confused expression on his face. 'I thought I was done. Suddenly, I find I'm not. But, since you said on the plane that we should be honest about bedroom matters, I have to confess I am not a big fan of the missionary position. So would you mind if we tried something different?'

He didn't wait for her to say yes or no. He just sat up, pulling Megan up into a sitting position as well. Taking hold of her knees, he slid her thighs on top of his, then hooked her legs around his back, whilst his were spreadeagled on the bed in front of him.

Before she could blink, he'd pushed himself deep inside her.

'This isn't the easiest position for the man to move in, mind,' he growled as he took her hips captive in his hands. 'I don't have much leverage. You'll have to do some of the work. With your insides. Grip me tight as I rock you back and forth. Yes, that's the way. Aah, yes…see how good you are at this? God, that feels fantastic. You like it, too. I can see that you do.'

Like it? What kind of understatement was that? She *loved* it.

But she wanted more.

'Kiss me,' she demanded.

James thrilled to Megan's passionate demand. This was what he wanted in his wife. A woman with needs that matched his own. He'd never thought that Megan would measure up in that regard; that she was capable of giving him the degree of pleasure he'd experienced with Jackie.

But he'd been wrong. Megan promised to be an even more exciting partner. The prospect of teaching her everything he knew was incredibly exciting. On top of that, he would never have to look back and think that anything Megan did for him was fake. Her pleasure was real, her love was real...*she* was real.

He reached up to cup her face and kiss her, revelling in the hunger of her lips and her tongue. Her hips kept moving of their own accord, their rhythm almost frantic, her flesh clenching and unclenching around his. His climax took his breath away, his mouth wrenching away from hers as a raw cry burst from his lungs. For a split second he thought he was having a heart attack, his chest constricting tightly, as if there were a vice around it. But then she came too, and there was nothing but pleasure. Wave after wave of it. Glorious, rapturous, mind-blowing pleasure!

James was just beginning to come back to reality when he felt Megan's mouth, warm and wet against his neck. He glanced down to see that she'd nestled into him, her arms now wrapped tightly around his back, her still parted lips pressed against his skin.

Her sigh was the sigh of a contented woman.

That sigh gave him more satisfaction than anything he'd ever heard. If anyone in this world deserved to be content, it was Megan. All she needed now, James believed, was to conceive a baby. Hopefully, in a week's time, he would be able to give her that as well.

Meanwhile...

He didn't move for another couple of minutes, by which time it became obvious that Megan had fallen asleep. Very carefully, he laid her back on the bed before even more carefully withdrawing. His yawn told him he was pretty tired himself. Sleep seemed not only attractive but also imperative if he was to keep this up.

What next could he try with her? James wondered as his mind began to drift.

The possibilities were, indeed, endless...

CHAPTER NINE

JAMES woke before Megan. For a long while he just lay there on his side, looking at her and thinking how lucky he was to have married her. At one stage she rolled over and snuggled up to him in her sleep, her bare breasts pressing against his chest.

When he felt his flesh stir James considered waking her and making love to her again. But a glance at the bedside clock showed that it was getting on for five-thirty and the light outside was fading. Better he leave her to rest for now.

Very carefully he eased himself away from temptation. She didn't wake, just made a small moan then curled herself up into a foetal position. James threw a sheet over her rather provocative nakedness, then hurried through the living room and out onto the wooden deck which surrounded the pool. The solar-heated water, however, was perhaps a little too warm for what he wanted, so he ran down the narrow sandy path which led to the beach, plunging straight into the sea, where the cooler water thankfully succeeded in taming his wayward flesh.

James didn't like the idea of sitting through a meal in a restaurant later this evening with a hard-on. Still, he wouldn't book that à la carte restaurant which their guide had raved about, the one on the top floor of the hotel. It took hours to eat in places like that, the service always slow, with the courses well spaced out. You were also expected to drink lots of wine.

There were times when James enjoyed that kind of thing. But not tonight. Tonight he wanted to get Megan back here at a reasonable hour, with himself still sober. Though it wouldn't matter if she was a bit tipsy.

Megan was still fast asleep when he walked into the bedroom, dripping wet from his swim. Fortunately most of the floors in the villa were polished timber, so he wasn't creating too much of a mess. Still, he headed straight for the bathroom, where he showered but didn't shave, despite a five o'clock shadow having appeared. From now on—or for at least the duration of this holiday—James planned to deliver a different lover to Megan from the highly conservative bed partner he'd been up till now.

Megan was still sound asleep when James emerged from the bathroom, his refreshed body now wrapped in one of the white towelling bathrobes which had been hanging on the back of the bathroom door.

Poor little love, he thought as he walked over to the bed and stared down at her. She must be exhausted, what with the travelling and all that raunchy sex. He suspected, however, that Megan was suffering a degree of emotional exhaustion as well. Making decisions and changes in one's life sometimes came at a price. James knew this only too well, his own life's journey not being as smooth or as silver-tailed as some people thought, given his father was a billionaire.

What people hadn't known was that his father was a pig and a controlling bully who'd abused his wife and had his two sons' lives all mapped out for them from birth. James's older brother, Jonathon, had gone along with their domineering parent—up to a point. But James had always been strong-minded and rebellious, and had often been punished the same way the whole family was always punished when they dared to go against Wayne Logan's will: first with his father's fists, and then, when James had been big enough to fight back, by the withdrawal of his father's financial support.

If it hadn't been for the money Jonathon had left him when he died, James would never have been able to afford to study law at university. Not straight away after leaving school. His father had given him an ultimatum on the night of his graduation, just a week before Jonathon's car accident. Either come into the family business, or he was out on his own. James had chosen to go it alone, even before he'd inherited his brother's estate, which included an apartment in the middle of the city and a portfolio of stocks and shares which would provide an income whilst he got his degree.

Consequently, his father no longer spoke to him, not even when James had come to visit his dying mother in hospital a few years back. Every time James had walked into the room, his father walked out, uncaring of how this might affect his long-suffering wife. He hadn't attended either of James's weddings, either.

There again, James had never invited him.

Jackie knew the truth. James had been foolish enough to tell her everything, as one did when one was madly in love. Not so Megan, who had been told his widowed father now lived overseas—which he did—and wasn't well enough to travel. When no wedding present arrived, James had made the excuse that his father wasn't one to send gifts, because his wife had always done that for him.

Strangely, the Press had never cottoned on to their estrangement. Wayne Logan always praised his successful son to the media. And James cleverly avoided the subject of his father.

For a long time, James hadn't wanted marriage and a family. Bad examples could do that to you. After his mother passed away, however, he'd begun to change his mind, slowly becoming obsessed with the idea of being a good husband and father. When he'd fallen in love with Jackie, he hadn't been able to wait to prove that he could be both.

James supposed it was just as well Jackie had been unable to have children. She would have made a rotten mother.

Megan, however, he thought with a wave of tenderness, would be wonderful. She didn't have a mean bone in her body. Neither was she empty or vain or materialistic. She was sweet and warm and loving. He'd felt terribly sorry for her when she'd lost their baby, but who knew? Maybe it would be all for the best in the end. They said that what didn't kill you made you stronger.

Megan had finally emerged from her grief last week a much stronger person. James had great respect for anyone who could overcome adversity and not sit around forever, indulging in self-pity and suffering from the 'why me?' syndrome, which Megan had been in real danger of doing.

Not any longer, however.

James was suddenly tempted to wake her so that he could tell her how much he admired her today. But he didn't. His compliment might get misinterpreted as a lead-in to more sex. Given he was suddenly finding the new Megan almost irresistible in that department, and that he wanted to save himself for later, James erred on the side of caution and let her sleep on.

Instead, he set about keeping himself busy. First, he checked the message bank on his mobile phone. Nothing, thank goodness. He didn't think Megan would be too impressed with him doing business whilst on their second honeymoon. Still, he didn't turn it off. Who knew when he might be needed?

The new casting agency he'd set up at Images was still very much in the development stage. He'd instructed the capable but relatively inexperienced staff there not to hesitate to call him if they wanted a second opinion. He supposed that was unlikely over the weekend, but things could hot up next week.

They'd recently secured the job of casting a rather important movie and they just might need to run something by him.

Next, he rang Reception and booked a table for seven-thirty that evening at one of the resort's more casual restaurants—the Hibiscus. Apparently it had a varied menu, ranging from seafood to Asian dishes. The service was reputedly quick and one didn't have to dress up. Just the thing.

After that, he unpacked, not only his case, but also Megan's, his eyebrows arching at the clothes she'd brought with her. All obviously new and all super-sexy. There was a teeny-weeny red bikini which he couldn't wait to see on her.

When Megan still wasn't awake at six-thirty, he almost gave her a shake, but decided to get himself dressed first, choosing his clothes with care. Loose beige linen trousers, a long-sleeved black silk shirt, which he rolled up to the elbows. Black belt and beige Italian loafers. He was standing by the bed and slipping his gold Rolex back onto his wrist when he became aware that Megan's eyes were open.

'Well, well, well,' he said smilingly. 'Sleeping Beauty has returned to the land of the living.'

'You're dressed,' she said.

'Sorry, darling, but I really can't go out in my birthday suit.'

'Out?' she echoed, as though he were talking in a foreign language.

James sighed, then decided it was time for the facts-of-life talk.

'As much as hopping back into bed with you is very appealing,' he said, 'unfortunately, once a man passes thirty-five his mind has much more stamina than his flesh. It would be heaven to make love to you all day every day, but I'm afraid I'm going to have to take some breaks occasionally. Sad, I know, but true. Given I'm not much into takeaway food or picnics, I thought dinner out each night would be just the ticket. After all,' he added with a wry smile, 'if we never go out, when are you going to wear all those sexy little dresses you brought with you?'

Megan's mouth fell open. 'You unpacked my things?'

'Don't sound so surprised. I always pack and unpack my own case when I go away. I'll have you know that I can also cook, clean, wash and iron. When I have to.' Fortunately, he hadn't had to do any of those things for many years. James could not think of anything more boring than housework. He liked the luxury of having staff do what he disliked doing himself.

'Where did you put my toiletries?' Megan asked.

'In the bathroom, of course.'

'You didn't unpack it as well, did you?'

'Good lord, no. I understand that a woman's toilet bag is no fit place for a man to venture. So your feminine secrets are safe,' he added with a smile as he glanced at his watch. 'Look, it's just after six-thirty. Our booking at the restaurant is for seven-thirty. That gives you about forty-five minutes to be ready. Can you manage in that time?'

Her hand lifted to run through her decidedly messy hair. 'I'll have to put my hair up. It takes ages to blow-dry this layered cut properly.'

'Do it like it was done last Monday morning. It looked very sexy like that.'

And *you* look very sexy, Megan thought as she stared back at her husband.

The saying that 'clothes maketh the man' did not apply to James. He made the clothes, in her opinion. There was nothing he didn't look good in. A combination, she supposed, of his height and body shape, along with his way of standing, always upright with his shoulders back, his chest out and his stomach tucked in. His walk was attractive as well, his stride long and confident, drawing attention to his lean hips and tight butt. Or it did when he was wearing jeans, or those slim-cut trousers he always wore to golf.

Tonight, he was wearing loosely tailored trousers and a shiny black shirt she'd never seen before. The top two buttons were open and the sleeves rolled up to his elbows, showing the tan he'd acquired over the summer. His short hair was still slightly damp, suggesting a recent shower. But he hadn't shaved, which was not like James. He usually shaved twice a day, being prone to obvious five o'clock shadow.

James had never gone in for the designer-stubble look, but she could see that it suited him, the same way his short hair-style suited him. When both were combined with that slick black shirt, he looked not just sexy, she realised, but danger-ous too.

As her eyes travelled over him, her belly tightened and her heartbeat quickened, images filling her mind of what they'd done earlier. She wanted to experience it all again. Quite des-perately. Right now. If only he hadn't made that stupid res-taurant booking.

Oh, my God!

'What time did you say it was?' she suddenly choked out.

'It's just gone six-thirty.'

'I'd better get going, then,' she said and, jumping out of bed, Megan bolted for the bathroom. She always took her pill around six o'clock, a time she'd chosen because she'd been sure of being awake—and reasonably alert—at six in the evening. Since her miscarriage the mornings had not been her best time for remembering anything, her depression at its peak in the hours she was first awake.

If she'd been taking a normal pill, it wouldn't have mattered if she took it an hour or two later. But she was on the mini-pill, the doctor warning her that she should be careful to take it at approximately the same time every day.

After locking the bathroom door, Megan hurried to extract her pills from her toilet bag, washing one quickly down with a glass of water before jamming the packet out of sight in an inside pocket. She shuddered to think what might have happened if James had decided to take all her toiletries out of her bag. He'd have surely seen the packet of pills which she hadn't thought to hide.

That would have been a disaster!

No way would he have been smiling at her out there if he had. He'd have hit the roof.

'I'll be as quick as I can,' Megan called back through the door.

'Fine,' James replied. 'I'll go and watch the TV.'

Megan breathed a sigh of relief, glad to have some time alone to gather herself. And to think about what had happened since they'd arrived here today.

Megan had always known James was a good lover. But he was more than good, she realised. He was wicked. A perfectionist in everything he did, he'd obviously learned all the right moves, and all the right positions for giving the maximum amount of physical pleasure.

Clearly, from what he'd said earlier, he didn't count the missionary position as one of those.

Not that she hadn't always enjoyed making love with James in the missionary position. She had. She'd especially liked that you could look into each other's eyes and hold each other close. It was the position of true love and romance.

What James had been doing to her today, and what he promised to do to her in the future, had nothing to do with true love, or romance. It was all about sex. Wildly addictive and ultimately corrupting sex. Already she could think of nothing else.

With another shudder—this one far more erotic—she switched on the nearest shower head, her eyes automatically going to the tiles on the back wall as she stepped under the warm spray of water. She could see herself now, pressed up against them, one leg up and her mouth gaping wide as she came. When she reached for the shower gel, she remembered what James had done with it afterwards, the way he'd rubbed it all over her breasts, and then down between her legs. She found herself doing the same, reliving the experience, feeling her nipples harden as they had back then. Slowly, inexorably, her hands travelled downwards, her breath catching as the tension built up in her body.

Just in time she stopped, knowing instinctively that any climax she gave herself simply would not compare. She would save her excitement for him. Save herself for him.

Megan quickly switched off the water, stepped out of the shower and snatched up a towel. Once dry, she cleaned her teeth, then put her hair up the way James had said he liked. Once her make-up was done she stepped back and stared at her naked self in the mirror, her eyes travelling slowly from top to toe, lingering.

You do look sexy like that, Megan.

Now, what are you going to wear, sexy?

She had, as James had noted, bought several new dresses to wear here. All sexy in their own way, showing off quite a deal of skin and in bright, bold colours. But one stood out from all the rest.

It was red, a deep scarlet red, made in a soft, silky material which didn't crush. The style was the latest in this year's summer fashion, with a high waist and a short, swishy skirt. The neckline was very low-cut and the shoulder straps very thin. Megan had bought red high heels to go with it, along with red satin underwear, the strapless bra only half-cups and the panties a provocative thong. Naturally, she wasn't going to wear stockings.

All in all, it was just the outfit to wear, if you wanted to make sure your man got you home as soon as possible for afters.

So yes, *definitely* the red!

CHAPTER TEN

'RED suits you,' James said.

'Thank you,' Megan replied. 'It's not a colour I usually wear. I used to think it was too in-your-face. But Nicole talked me into it.'

They were on their way to the restaurant in the beach buggy, night having fallen and the narrow, winding road slightly more hazardous than it had been earlier on, despite lights hanging off the palm trees at intervals. The buggy lurched around the corners, setting Megan's earrings swinging. They were long drops of crystal, chosen for their match-anything non-colour.

'We use red a lot in ads,' James told her. 'It's the strongest of the primary colours. A recent survey actually proved that men found women more attractive in red than any other colour. They dressed the same woman in lots of different colours and most men voted her more attractive in red.'

'Really? Well, that's good. Because I bought a red bikini as well.'

'So I noticed. I'm looking forward to seeing you in it as well. And out of it,' he added with a wicked little smile.

Megan felt its effect right down to her freshly painted red toenails.

'With or without shoes,' she countered.

His sexy laugh made her heart zing and her belly tighten

at the same time. 'I'm not sure you'd survive wearing *those* shoes for too long,' he said, nodding towards the five-inch-high heels she was wearing.

'They're a bit much, aren't they?' she agreed.

'Hell, no. They're great. Just hard to walk in, I would imagine.'

'I've been practising.'

His sidewards glance carried amusement. 'Practice does make perfect. I'll let you practise on me later tonight.'

Megan's tongue suddenly felt thick in her mouth. 'Do…doing what?'

How delightful she was, James thought. Trying so hard to be saucy, when underneath she was still basically the same sweet, innocent girl he'd married. He loved it that she was now willing to try new things. But he also loved it that she'd never done any of those things with any other man.

Such thinking evoked a tender possessiveness towards her that he'd never felt before.

'Whatever you'd like to practise, my darling,' he replied softly.

When he slanted a quick glance her way, he caught her licking her lips. So *that* was what she wanted to do. He'd hoped as much.

Just the thought of it, however, was painful. He would really have to get off the subject of sex for a while.

The sight of the security gate ahead heralded the end of the private road, James acknowledging the guard with a nod as he waved them through. The rainforest on either side ended abruptly at that point, replaced by the more ordered gardens which surrounded the resort buildings. There were also a lot more roads, going in all directions. White signposts at each intersection indicated which way to go to find the hotel, the main beach, the pools and yes, there it was, the Hibiscus!

James swung the buggy to the left and followed the road round to the restaurant's car park, which was surprisingly full.

He'd heard that Dream Island was rarely empty, but he hadn't expected it to be this busy. Just as well he'd booked.

The restaurant had a wonderful ambience, with plate-glass windows on three sides which overlooked a terrace surrounding one of the largest pools James had ever seen. He'd been given a choice over the phone between outside and inside dining and had chosen inside, not sure whether to trust the weather at this time of the year. He'd been warned that the island occasionally suffered from wind gusts. He was now glad that he hadn't chosen to dine alfresco, the sea breeze stronger here than back at their villa. There was nothing worse in his opinion than food getting cold before you could eat it.

They were shown to a table which still had a splendid view of the pool, their handsome young waiter being very attentive as he took their drinks order, bringing the bottle of wine back to their table with a speed which James had found pleasing, till he noted the direction of the waiter's eyes.

He watched, highly irritated, when the waiter took his time opening and pouring the wine, his avid blue eyes returning to Megan's cleavage more times than was either polite or decent. OK, so Megan *was* a delectable dish tonight, and her full, creamy breasts were one of her best assets. But that didn't give this guy the right to ogle them.

If he stares at Megan's cleavage once more, James thought angrily by the time the waiter had finished setting up the wine in a portable ice buckct next to their table, I'll...I'll...

You'll *what*? the voice of savage reason piped up in his head. Create a scene? Hit the silly fool? Demand another table? Storm out?

James never acted like that. He'd spent his entire adult life exercising an iron control over his temper. Seeing the way his father had used to flare up over nothing, acting out anger with violence and frustration with verbal abuse, had made James determined never to resort to that kind of ugly and ultimately irrational behaviour. He'd gained a reputation over the years for his cool manner under pressure, and in a crisis. He never erupted, even when people did stupid things. He always remained in control.

He had never, ever surrendered to jealousy, not even when he'd been married to one of the most beautiful women in the world.

So it was a shock to find himself being subject to jabs of jealousy which were not only alien to him, but also increasingly difficult to control. The temptation to jump up and drag Megan out of here, away from the waiter's lecherous eyes, was intense.

She's for my eyes only, he suddenly wanted to scream.

How he gave him his meal order in a civil voice he had no idea. When Megan dithered over her choice, however, giving the serial ogler another opportunity to stare down her front, James had to do something before he exploded.

Quite deliberately, and with a great effort of will, he looked away from the sight provoking him, pretending to glance around the restaurant, as one did, though not really seeing anything till he became aware that the waiter had left their table with Megan's meal order.

Only then did his mind clear along with his eyes. So it was with a degree of surprise that his gaze encountered someone he knew sitting at a nearby table.

'Good lord, it's Jessie!' he exclaimed.

Jessie must have heard her name, for she looked up, smiled, then waved. Though she was still a client of the management side of Images, James hadn't been personally involved with his biggest success story in some years. Once Jackie had come on the scene, he thought it best if he handed his former lover's management over to another agent, a consideration which had probably been wasted. But he hadn't known that at the time.

Jessie was still doing reasonably well on the club circuit. Still earning a good living. But she no longer commanded the kind of fees and CD sales which she once had. Of course, she was well over forty now. But she still looked damned good. She hadn't let herself go, her figure remaining trim and her face relatively unlined. Admittedly, the lighting in the restaurant was not overly bright, so perhaps she would look older up close. On the stage, however, she would still look great.

He waved back to her, than glanced over at Megan, who was sipping her wine and looking a little flushed. That she might have enjoyed being ogled by that waiter annoyed the hell out of him. Suddenly, he wasn't sure if he liked her new sexy image after all!

'You'll have to excuse me for a moment, Megan,' he said, his voice sounding much calmer than he felt. 'I must go say hello to a good friend of mine.'

Megan stiffened at this unexpected development. She'd been rather enjoying the waiter's attention; had even thought she saw a hint of jealousy in James's eyes. It had excited her to think he might be jealous. Jealousy often meant caring, didn't it?

Now, suddenly, she was the jealous one. For she knew exactly who James meant. 'I presume you're talking about Jessica Mason over there,' Megan said, somewhat tartly.

James stared over at her. 'You're a fan of Jessie's?'

'For pity's sake, James, everyone knows the infamous Jessie. And what you did for her. It was in all the newspapers and glossies for ages.' Neither of which she'd used to read back then. If she hadn't looked James up on the internet, she'd never have known a thing about his association with Jessica Mason, or his past life. He never talked about it. Never told her a darned thing.

But why should he? she thought with a sudden burst of bitterness. She wasn't his soulmate. Just his silly second wife. And now his silly sex slave as well.

Dear God, what a fool she was!

'But that was years ago,' he argued.

Megan shrugged. 'I think I was alive at the time. And able to read. I am almost twenty-five, James, not five.'

'I see.'

'Why don't you invite her to join us?' Megan heard herself saying. Lord knew why. She had to be a masochist. Or was it curiosity which had evoked the offer, a wanting to see the woman up close, to see if she did really look as fabulous as she did from a distance?

'You don't mind?'

'Should I?'

'No,' he said somewhat hesitantly. 'I guess not.'

Hardly a reassuring reply. But she just smiled and James hurried off to invite his past conquest over to their table.

For no way did he not sleep with her, Megan thought as the woman rose and walked towards the table, her walk as sensual as her face and figure. Dressed as she was in tight black jeans and an extremely low-cut yellow knitted top, everything was on open display.

She's probably had a boob job, Megan thought bitchily as she was confronted by the woman's double-D-size cups. And a facelift. For even up close, there weren't too many lines on her striking-looking face, not even around her eyes. Admittedly, she did have a lot of make-up on. Too much, in Megan's opinion. Her extra-long, very black curly hair was also much too young for her, and just a little harsh. Though not, perhaps, at night. But Megan could imagine that in the daylight, she would look like mutton dressed up as lamb.

'No, no, James,' the woman herself said when he went to pull up an extra chair. 'I won't be staying. I've finished my meal and I must get going. I'm singing in the main lounge up at the hotel tonight. I just wanted to come over and wish you and your pretty wife all the best of luck. I'd heard you married again last year. You seem to have chosen better the second time round,' she added, startling Megan with her warm smile.

'Lovely to meet you, my dear,' she added, and extended her right hand.

'Same here,' Megan said, and shook it.

'Your husband is a wonderful man, you know,' Jessie went on. 'He helped me when I desperately needed help. I will for ever be grateful to him. No, James, do sit down and shut up for once. Men!' she directed towards Megan with exasperation in her voice. 'They simply do not know how to take a compliment. Anyway, sweet things, I must away. If you have the time you should come and hear me sing later tonight. I go on at nine, and eleven as well. Have to make it tonight, though, as I'm off back to Melbourne tomorrow. This was just a short gig. Of course, I will understand if you don't. I do understand that people come here for things other than gadding about.'

'Megan and I are having a second honeymoon,' James informed her.

'How romantic! James must love you a lot, my dear. Because I wouldn't say romance is his forte.'

'What happened to the compliments?' James said drily.

'James, darling, I would imagine that Megan here already knows what a pragmatist you are. And it's no crime not to be a romantic. I've always found that the most romantic men are usually sleazebags in disguise. Give me someone brutally honest like you are any day of the week. Now I really must go. It's been lovely catching up. Ta-ta,' she said, and with a final wave was off.

Megan just sat there after she left, drinking in everything Jessie had said, and doing her best not to feel both bitter and jealous at the same time. For not only had James slept with that woman, but he was also honest with her.

If only he'd been honest with me, Megan wailed inside. If only he'd told me the truth. That all he wanted from me was a child. I might still have been stupid enough to marry him, but at least I'd have known the truth.

Their meals arrived without her saying a word, not even thank you to the waiter. Once he was gone she stared down at what she'd ordered, surprised to find that it was a risotto. She couldn't remember what flavour, but it looked like chicken and mushroom, with a bit of spinach thrown in. Or something else that was green.

James's meal was a huge rump steak and salad.

He didn't pick up his knife and fork straight away either, instead giving her a thoughtful look.

'What's wrong?' he asked.

'Nothing,' she lied, and picked up her wine glass instead of a fork.

'There's no need to be jealous of Jessie,' he said, his intuitive remark sparking anger.

'Why's that? Because you haven't slept with her for a few years?'

James could not help being pleased by the tartness of her remark. More than pleased. He felt soothed.

Strange, his own jealousy had bothered him greatly. Not so Megan's. He liked hers. A lot.

'I didn't love Jessie,' he said.

Megan almost laughed. What's new? she wanted to say. You don't love any woman you sleep with. Or even marry.

'That's not the point,' she said irritably.

'Then what is the point?'

'The point is she knows you better than I do,' Megan snapped. 'You never talk to me, James. And yes, I know there hasn't been much talking since I lost the baby. And I suppose that's my fault. But you didn't talk to me even before that. Not really. I would know absolutely nothing about your past, or your career, or that bloody woman, if I hadn't looked you up on the internet.'

James was totally taken aback, both by Megan's hot temper and her revelation. 'You looked me up on the internet?'

'How else would I have found out who and what you

were? I was madly in love with you but I didn't know you. I still don't know you. Like I said, Jessica Mason knows you better than I do.'

'Not really.'

'How can you say that? You worked with her for a long time. And you were lovers. Don't deny it.'

'I haven't denied it.'

'How nice that your brutal honesty only goes so far!'

James frowned. 'What do you mean by that?'

'Nothing,' she bit out, and picked up her fork.

'No, you meant something.'

Now is your opportunity, Megan. Tell him. Tell him you know he doesn't love you. That he's lied to you all along.

But she just couldn't.

Was it her lust for him which stopped her? Or the love she still felt?

Maybe both.

Her sigh carried a measure of frustration. 'The thing is, James, a wife wants to understand her husband, not just love him like a blind fool. You should have shared more of your past life with me. I told you *everything* about myself. Not that there was all that much. No incredible life experiences. No newsworthy successes. Certainly no previous lovers to confess to.'

'But you never wanted to know about my past girlfriends,' he protested. 'You told me so.'

Perhaps because subconsciously I was afraid to know, Megan realised with a flash of insight. Who wants to hear about super-beautiful, super-glamorous women that your husband had been with? Especially when you're just a very ordinary girl with no special beauty or talents to speak of.

But she wasn't afraid any more, came another unexpected realisation. If nothing else, this past week had shown her that she had the courage to speak up. About some things, anyway.

'I'm not talking just about your love life, James,' Megan

said, 'but your life! What were you like as a child? What were your hopes and your fears? Your dreams and your ambitions?'

James felt some exasperation at this third degree from Megan. He'd never been partial to telling his life story. Reminiscing over his wretched upbringing was not his idea of fun. But he could see her point. He hadn't been very forth-coming with her, a hangover perhaps of having told Jackie everything, then finding out he'd revealed his very soul to a creature without a soul herself.

He could see, however, how much it meant to Megan to know some more about him.

So he told her, over their meal, about his family life, and about his father. He held nothing back. He told the truth, warts and all. It wasn't till he came to the part about his brother's death that he felt his throat tighten. He managed to tell Megan about his brother's will, but then he simply had to stop.

Scooping in a deep, gathering breath, he picked up his wine glass, downed it all in one gulp, then exhaled slowly.

This is why I don't like talking about the past, James accepted ruefully. Because I can't stand the painful memories. Can't stand the pain.

Megan stared at her husband. She'd listened, horrified, to the tale of his family's abuse at the hands of a brutal father. His stories of being beaten and bullied made her own com-plaints about her materialistic and slightly domineering mother seem small, and insignificant. Megan had never doubted that her mother loved her. Neither did her father really mind that his wife nagged him. Henry Donnelly was a soft-hearted but rather silly man who needed a practical and forceful woman to keep his life in order. Forceful, but never cruel.

It came to Megan that James's inability to love might have come from the lack of love in his childhood. How could you ever show what you were never shown? Maybe if his brother had lived things might have been different. Jonathon must have loved his little brother a lot to leave him everything in his will.

'How old was Jonathon when he died?' she asked, unable to remember from the newspaper article.

'Twenty-three. The coroner declared it an accident,' James said with a wry twist to his lips. 'A combination of speed and alcohol. But I've always thought it odd that Jonathon only made his will the day before he died, leaving everything to me. Prior to that he didn't have a will at all. Why that day, I ask myself?'

'You think he *killed* himself?'

James shrugged. 'I don't know. No one knows, except perhaps my father. I do know this: Jonathon wasn't happy. He was a very smart guy. Had an IQ of 150. He wanted to be a doctor. But Dad refused to pay for him to go to medical school. So he went into the family business and became dad's lackey. A well-paid lackey, obviously, by the size of his estate, but still a lackey.'

'He could have left and been his own man, James, the way you did.'

'It wasn't as easy as that. Jonathon was the first-born, the more responsible son. He didn't stay at home because he was afraid to leave. He stayed to protect our mother.'

'Oh, James. That's simply tragic.'

The sympathy in her eyes and voice touched him. But he didn't really want it. Neither did he want to talk any more about the subject of his father. Or his past.

'Could we leave any more sharing of my life story to some other time?' he said abruptly. 'We'll have that infernal waiter coming over soon and asking me if there's anything wrong with the food, just so he can stare down your cleavage. We won't be coming here again, that's for sure, not with you dressed like that.'

'I'm no more provocatively dressed than your Jessie was,'

Megan defended herself, whilst feeling secretly pleased with James's jealousy.

'Jessie's not my wife. I don't care if she likes being ogled by strangers.'

Megan gasped. 'I do not like being ogled by strangers. How dare you say that?'

James smiled. He dared because he wanted to get back to the very subject he'd vowed to avoid earlier. Sex was a wonderful distraction for emotional distress. Or so he'd always found, right from his youngest days.

'You look very beautiful when you're angry,' he said. 'Now, eat up your risotto.'

Megan glared at him, hating the way he could accuse her of something distasteful, then immediately attempt to disarm her with such a clichéd and manipulative compliment. As sorry as she'd felt for him a minute ago, she now felt nothing but anger.

'I'm not hungry any more,' she said mutinously.

'Neither am I,' he replied, then stared hard, first at her face, then at her breasts, then back at her mouth. 'At least…not for food,' he added, a wild glitter in his dark eyes.

Megan sucked in sharply. This was what could disarm her. Having him look at her like that.

'Let's get out of here,' he suggested thickly. 'Right now.'

Megan swallowed. 'But…but what about the rest of our food? And the wine?'

'There's food back at the villa. And loads of wine.'

She just stared at him. Did she dare do this? Just get up and leave? It seemed outrageous. But ooh, she wanted to.

'Don't think,' he commanded gruffly as he stood up then reached for her hand. 'Just leave everything and come with me.'

For a split second Megan still hesitated, her survival instinct warning her that if she put her hand in his, if she obeyed him without question, then she would be lost. He would run rampant with her body, and her life. There would be no possibility of leaving him. She would become his as she'd never been before.

Was it the rampant hunger in his eyes which swayed her? Or what he'd confided to her earlier? Who could say what it was that sealed her fate?

Megan stood up somewhat shakily, then stretched out her hand.

CHAPTER ELEVEN

JAMES could not believe the buzz he got when she placed her hand in his. Yes, he thought triumphantly. *Yes!*

His fingers closed tightly around hers, his heart thudding loudly in his chest as he almost dragged her across the tiled floor of the restaurant, past the bulging eyes of their waiter, out of the door, then over to the car park.

They were in the buggy and on their way in no time flat. The beach buggy, however, was not a speedy vehicle. James had to slow even further at the security gate, waving at the guard before accelerating along the winding track that would lead them back to the villa and straight to bed.

Thinking about making love catapulted James back to the dangerous state he'd been in earlier when that lecherous bastard had been ogling Megan's breasts. No, that was an understatement. He was worse now. Much worse. Hell on earth, he'd never had an erection like it. The road suddenly seemed endless. He could not wait. He simply could not wait.

Megan gasped when James muttered a sexually based expletive, then pulled the already lurching buggy over to the side of the road, his applying of the brakes so fierce that she almost fell out. She had no time to ask him what was wrong before he scooped her up off the leather seat and carried her into the darkened forest.

'I can't wait' were the only words he spoke to her.

They were enough. Megan knew what he was going to do. Knew she was going to let him.

The palm tree he leant her up against had a wide trunk, and was leaning slightly backwards. He didn't undress either himself or her. He unzipped his trousers then lifted her skirt, pushing aside the thin strip of red satin which was the only barrier between his flesh and hers.

Megan cried out when he drove up into her, a sharp keening sound rather like that of a bird. After that she was quiet, for his mouth had swooped to silence her, muffling the moans which tried to escape from her throat. Her head spun with the wild savagery of his mating, Megan thrilling to the intensity of his passion for her. He came much too quickly for her, but she still loved it. She especially loved the way he held her to him afterwards, as if he was a drowning man, and she his lifeline.

'Sorry,' he muttered into her hair. 'Sorry.'

His apology surprised her.

'No need to apologise,' she whispered in the darkness. 'I didn't mind.'

'There's every need,' he growled. 'I acted like some wild animal.'

'But I really didn't mind,' she insisted.

His head lifted and she could feel him staring down at her in the darkness.

'You're telling me the truth? You're not just saying that?'

For an answer she reached up to cup his face with tender hands. 'I would never lie to you,' she murmured.

He groaned, then kissed her again, kissed her till she felt his flesh twitch inside her own.

'Next time will be for you, my darling,' he said against her lips, then hoisted her up onto his hips.

Amazingly he carried her back to the buggy like that, after which, even more amazingly, he drove back to the villa with her sitting in his lap, facing him, their bodies still fused. The road was not all that smooth, and by the time James parked the buggy under its carport Megan's focus was on one thing and one thing only: release from the screaming sexual tension which was gripping her body. When he started walking from the buggy to the villa, she buried her face into the base of his throat and prayed for a speedy deliverance. When he didn't carry her straight inside, her head shot up, just in time to see where they were and what he was about to do.

'No, don't!' she cried out as he walked slowly down the steps into the pool. 'You'll ruin our clothes!'

'I doubt it. Expensive clothes don't ruin that easily.'

The water gradually encircled them both, deliciously warm and sensuous. But their clothes soon became a problem, James's shirt glued to his chest, whilst Megan's skirt floated up onto the surface.

'I think we'd better get naked,' James said.

'But…' She didn't want to separate from him.

'Yes, I know,' he said, 'but it's just a short interruption. We have all night, Megan. In fact, we have ten whole days.'

Taking clothes off in a pool was not easy, she discovered. Finally they were both naked, only her earrings remaining, along with his gold Rolex. She swam back towards him from the side of the pool, the water moving over her naked flesh like a silken glove, caressing and arousing.

'I think we should get out now.'

'What? But why?'

'Making love in water is a common fantasy. But it can be a bit of an anticlimax. I only came in here to cool us both down. You stay whilst I go and get you something cosy to put on.' He levered himself out of the pool in a flash and dashed across the decking, disappearing inside within seconds.

Megan could not help feeling disappointed, no matter what James said. She didn't think making love in the water would have been an anticlimax at all! Of course, he'd already had his climax, whereas she felt totally frustrated.

James came back, carrying one of the thick white towelling robes she'd seen hanging up on the back of the bathroom door. He himself had nothing on but a turquoise towel slung low around his hips.

'Come on, little mermaid. Out of there.'

Megan tried not to feel self-conscious as she made her way up the graduated steps of the pool; tried to be bold and not care that he was staring at her with annoyingly cool eyes.

Unfortunately she still hadn't mastered her woman-of-the-world act, diving into the robe straight away and wrapping the rather thick sash tightly around her waist.

'No, I don't think so, Megan,' James said, and pulled the sash undone so that the robe fell open again. 'I want to look at you whilst I dry your hair.' And so saying, he whipped the towel from his hips.

He took his time drying her hair, and yes, he looked at her. Often. At one stage he pushed the robe further back so that her erect nipples were exposed. Once, he stroked the towel down over them, causing her to sway dangerously from side to side.

His eyes narrowed immediately and he threw the towel away.

'Time, I think, for bed.'

'Bed?' she repeated, rather surprised at this. She'd been imagining that he would make love to her somewhere else. Out here perhaps, on one of the banana loungers, or in the huge living room, where there were any number of sofas. And rugs. Thick, exotic-looking rugs just made for having sex on.

'Yes, bed,' he repeated. 'Don't look so surprised. There is method in my madness.'

She didn't doubt it. Clearly the uncontrollable beast she'd encountered earlier on, and whom she'd rather liked, was gone, replaced by the cool man-of-the-world she knew oh, so well, and who would never do a thing without thinking it through.

James did not make a habit of being impulsive. He was as pragmatic as Jessie had said he was. The fact Megan had managed to make him lose control, even once, brought a measure of satisfaction.

'Let's go,' he said and, firmly taking her elbow, steered her back into the villa, and into the bedroom.

The bed was still unmade from their encounters earlier in the day, the pillows all over the place. James straightened the satin sheets, then arranged the six pillows in two rows, three up against the bed head, another three in front of them.

'Now, let's get this off you,' he said, and peeled the robe back from her shoulders, letting it drop to the floor. 'Lie down in the middle of the bed, with your head resting on the first lot of pillows.'

Megan didn't question her willingness to obey him. She did what he said. Because she wanted to.

When he bent down to retrieve something from the floor, her head lifted off the pillows, her breath catching as she watched him pull the sash through the side-loops of the robe. Once again, she knew what he was going to do before he did it.

'Lift your arms up above your head towards the bed head. No, not that far. Rest your hands together on the pillows. You can bend your elbows a little.'

Her eyes were wide on his as he wound the towelling belt round one wrist and then the other.

'Not too tight?' he asked her.

'No,' she replied breathlessly.

'I want you to be comfortable,' he said quietly as he worked.

At last he climbed off the bed and just stared down at her.

She couldn't see exactly what he'd done. Only *feel*. She couldn't move her wrists apart but there was a little forwards and backwards movement. Clearly he'd tied her wrists together with the belt first, then attached it to the bed head in some way.

'How delicious you look,' he said, his voice still cool but his body anything but.

She didn't feel delicious so much as unbearably excited and recklessly abandoned. She wanted him to keep looking at her. But she wanted him to touch her more.

'So...do you like it, my darling?' he asked her.

Like it? Impossible to describe her feelings with inadequate words such as *like*. Her world had been tipped off its axis with his tying her up, her breathing so fast she thought her heart might jump out of her chest.

She simply could not speak.

'Do you want me to untie you? I will if you want me to.'

Her eyes met his as her head went slowly from side to side on the pillow.

He smiled. 'I had a feeling you'd like it.'

He'd just lain down next to her on the bed, his right hand hovering over her uptilted breasts, when the phone beside the bed rang.

Megan turned horrified eyes its way.

'Don't answer it,' she managed to croak out.

'It won't take long.'

'Yes?' he said rather sharply down the line. 'What? No, no, there wasn't anything wrong with the food. Or the wine. My wife came over a little faint, so I brought her home straight away.' This, with a wicked wink her way. 'Thank you for ringing. Yes, I'm sure she'll be fine. She just needs a little lie-down and some tender loving care. Bye.'

He hung up, then turned to her with the slowest, sexiest smile she'd ever seen. 'And now,' he said, and moved to stretch out lazily beside her once more, 'let's get down to that tender loving care...'

CHAPTER TWELVE

'DO YOU realise, Megan,' James said as he bobbed up and down in the sea, 'that not once, during the past week, has my office rung me.'

'Absolutely shocking,' she replied with a straight face. 'However have they been able to cope without you?'

'You mock me, madam, at your peril.'

Megan laughed. How happy she felt. Well…fairly happy.

A week ago, any measure of happiness had seemed impossible. But a week on Dream Island was a long time, especially when you spent all day every day together. She'd come to know James better during that short time than during the whole of their marriage; come to accept that, whilst he might not love her the way Hugh loved his new bride, he did care about her. Their new intimacy—and she wasn't just talking about sex—went a long way to giving her some hope that their marriage was worth saving.

He hadn't confided any more about his wretched upbringing, but he had talked to her quite a bit about his work. She'd discovered that James had more of a creative mind than she'd previously thought. Megan had always believed that her pragmatic husband's successes had come from his business acumen. She'd gained the impression from his friends that he was the master of delegation. She knew now that he was actually a very hands-on person when it came to the ad campaigns that Images was famous for.

Which was perhaps why he was peeved that they hadn't contacted him over the past week. He obviously believed that Images could not survive without his presence, or at least his input, especially in reference to the casting agency he'd started up recently.

'You could always call them,' she told him.

'Humph!' He snorted. 'And when, pray tell, have I had the time to do anything around here except keep my wife satisfied?'

'You only have yourself to blame. You insisted on broadening my sexual horizons.'

'I've created a monster.'

'I didn't notice you not enjoying yourself this afternoon.'

Megan's heartbeat quickened at the memory of what she'd done to him. She might not have had any previous experience at performing oral sex—and she'd been much more nervous than she'd pretended to be—but once she saw the pleasure she was giving him, then everything had gone swimmingly.

His dark eyes glittered at her. 'For someone who's never done that before, you were amazingly good at it.'

She almost said she'd concentrated on her love for him, but didn't. That was one thing she hadn't been able to do on this getaway. Tell James that she loved him. Perhaps it was because she didn't want him saying it back to her. She could live with a husband who desired her. Which she now believed he did. But not one who lied to her.

Strangely, he hadn't said he loved her either, for which she was grateful. Megan wondered how she would react if and when he did say it to her again. She supposed she would just have to wait and see. Just as she would have to wait and see before she did anything impulsive like throw away her pills.

Having a baby could wait.

Which reminded her...

'What time is it?' she asked James.

'Around five-thirty.'

They'd taken to swimming in the sea late in the afternoon, the water lovely by then. Afterwards, they'd get dressed and drive into the resort for dinner. Last night they'd lingered a long time over a five-course meal in the hotel's main à la carte restaurant, James claiming he needed time and lots of food to restore his energy. They'd possibly drunk a little too much wine as well, because they'd both fallen asleep quite quickly after making love only the once on their return to the villa.

Today had been a different story. James had been ravenous for her all day, waking her early in the morning for the first of many lovemaking sessions. The only time he'd left her alone was mid-morning, when Housekeeping had come to clean the villa. And now, during their leisurely afternoon swim.

'We'll have to get out soon,' Megan said, thinking she didn't want to be late taking her pill.

'Good idea. I think I'm getting a headache. I've either had too much sun…or too much of something else,' he added with a rueful smile.

'Poor darling.'

'I'm a glutton for punishment,' he said with an air of mock-suffering. 'Look, I'll get out first. That way I won't be tempted on the walk back by the sight of you in that sexy red bikini.'

Megan loved the way he complimented her all the time. He made her feel really beautiful and extremely desirable.

'Do you have something you can take?' she asked, not wanting his headache to continue.

'There's sure to be some painkillers in the bathroom. It has everything else that opens and shuts.'

He was already heading for the shallows, the water level quickly dropping to his waist, then lower.

Megan stared at his naked backside, which was now sporting a mild tan. James never wore swimming trunks, almost becoming that nudist he'd suggested on their first day. He had a great body, she thought for the umpteenth time. A great everything, front and back.

'I hope you don't go using that headache as an excuse,' she called out to him as he strode up the palm-lined path which led back to the villa.

His head turned to throw a wry smile over his shoulder. 'Don't worry. I'll soldier on.'

Megan laughed, then began hauling herself out of the water as well. When she reached the villa, she jumped in the pool to wash the salt and sand off her body. And it was while she was stroking lazily up and down that James walked back out onto the deck, his nakedness now covered by one of the white bathrobes, his hands sunk deep in the pockets.

'Did you find some tablets?' she asked.

'I did indeed,' he replied in an oddly cold voice. 'But they weren't painkillers. Would you care to explain these?' he said, and pulled his right hand out of the pocket, stretching out his fingers to reveal her month's supply of the Pill.

Guilt was written all over her face, James saw immediately, making him feel even sicker than he had when he'd come across them.

There hadn't been any painkillers in the vanity-unit drawers, or on the shelves behind the mirror, his searching all through Megan's toilet bag a desperate last resort. He hadn't had a migraine for years, but the jagged circles dancing in front of his eyes indicated that he was about to suffer a bad one.

Finding that packet of pills had sent his head spinning further. He tried to stay calm, but he could feel a blind rage rising up within him, blood pounding in his temples like a ket-tledrum.

'You had no intention of trying for another baby, did you?' he bit out.

'Well, I...I...'

'*Did* you?' he roared at her.

He watched as her face went a bright red.

All day today, every time he made love to her, he'd been thinking about her conceiving a child. *Their* child. Up till now it had been an unlikely consequence, and in truth, over the past week, his original mission behind bringing Megan on a second honeymoon had not been a priority. He'd been totally blown away by his new sexy wife. But it had always been there, in the background. It was, after all, what he wanted more than anything.

Her deliberately stopping conception from happening brought back some very bad memories, along with a welter of infuriating emotions. He'd thought she was different from Jackie. But she wasn't. She was just as selfish. And just as cruel. She knew he wanted a child. Knew he'd been hoping that it would happen on this holiday. Yet she'd deliberately made that impossible. She'd said the other night that she would never lie to him. But she had. The worst possible lie, in his eyes.

'James, please,' she said, still looking horribly guilty. 'Let me explain.'

'Too late,' he snapped. 'There's nothing you can say that will excuse what you've done. You lied to me, Megan. And you deceived me. I can't stand lies and deception.' With that, he whirled and stormed back down the path to the beach, where he was in the process of ripping the packet of pills to pieces and throwing the shreds into the sea when a dripping wet Megan materialised next to him, no longer looking at all guilty, or chastened.

'*You* can't stand lies and deception!' she threw at him, her hands firmly planted on her hips. 'That's rich coming from you, James Logan. You've lied to me and deceived me from the first moment we met!'

James just stared at her.

'You *never* loved me,' she spat. 'You wanted a child and I

was the fool who was going to give it to you. You made me believe that you really loved me. But you never did. Not for a single moment.'

'Who told you that?' he demanded to know.

'No one *told* me. I overheard Hugh and Russell talking when I was in the hospital. They thought I was asleep. Trust me when I say they gave me a very full picture of why you'd married me.'

James groaned, his pounding head making it hard for him to think clearly. Dismay was his first reaction, but his second was confusion. 'If that's the case, then why didn't you leave me right then and there?'

'Now, isn't that just the sort of thing my wonderfully sensitive husband would say?' Megan's expression was one of utter disgust. 'Has it occurred to you that, at the time, I was so devastated that I was incapable of taking any action at all? I wanted to leave you. Trust me on that. But I just didn't have the courage. After I went to Hugh's wedding, however, leaving you was very much on my mind. Because I saw what true love looked like, and I didn't want to settle for anything less. I was about to ask you for a divorce in the car on the way home afterwards when you kissed me and...well...the moment sort of passed. Then, the next morning, when you kissed me again and suggested this second honeymoon, I thought...well, I thought...'

'You thought what?' he snapped. 'That you'd have your revenge first?'

He waited for her to deny it. But she didn't deny it. She didn't say a single word. Just stared at him with those big brown eyes of hers.

James did what he always did when he was hurt. He came out fighting.

'I get the picture,' he snarled. 'You wanted to use me like you thought I'd used you. Maybe even get me to fall in love with you. Oh, yes, I dare say that was part of your vengeful little agenda. I have to give you credit, Megan, you pulled out all the stops. The sexy new image. The willingness to try new things. So tell me, darling, when you went down on me yesterday, and I begged you not to stop, did that give you a thrill? I'll just bet it did!'

It pained James to think that her making love to him that way had not come from her love for him, but from hate. It pained him more than anything he could recall. Not even finding out the truth about Jackie had hurt this much.

But he refused to let her see his distress. Refused to let her go without defending himself.

'You're wrong to think that I married you just for a child,' he slammed back at her. 'OK, so I didn't love you. I admit it. I lied about that. At the time, I felt incapable of loving any woman. But I liked you very much and wanted to make a family with you. A family and a life. A *good* life, full of caring and commitment. From the moment I met you I haven't even looked at another woman, not even when you wouldn't give me sex for three months. I never meant to hurt you. But you, Megan,' he pointed out with true bitterness in his voice and in his face, 'you *meant* to hurt me when you agreed to come away with me on this second honeymoon. You meant to hurt and to destroy. But let me tell you this, my girl: it will take more than this to destroy me. Much more. Now, go and pack your things and get the hell out of my life before I do something I *will* regret.'

Megan opened her mouth to say something. *Anything.*

But the look on James's face stopped her in her tracks. He might not have ever loved her, but he hated her now. She could see it in his eyes. There would be no point in defending herself, or apologising, or trying to explain further why she'd done what she'd done. No point at all.

It was over. Their marriage was finally over.

'Well, what are you waiting for?' he snapped. 'I'm sure you can find a room in the main hotel. Then you can take the morning helicopter back to the mainland. There are several flights from Cairns to Sydney every day. I'm sure you'll get a seat on one of them. The key to the beach buggy is on the coffee table. Any fool can drive it. So take the bloody thing and just go!'

Still she could not move. Inside, she was beginning to shake.

'James, I...I...'

'No!' he roared. 'I don't want to hear what you have to say. And I don't want to see your sorry face ever again. Or any other part of you. So make sure you're out of the house by the time I get home. My lawyer will be in touch,' he finished, and with one final savage glare he whirled and stalked off into the sea.

Megan wanted to run after him, beg him to listen. But again, she knew to do so would be futile. Not only did he hate her, but he thought she hated him too. His twisted logic that she'd come here for revenge made a sick kind of sense. In a way, she wished she had. Wished she *did* hate him.

Megan turned and somehow made her way back to the villa. It didn't take her long to dress and pack, though her hands shook all the time. The thought of driving that buggy and arriving alone at the resort hotel horrified her. What would they think?

By the time she did just that, however, Megan was too depressed and despairing to care what they thought. She was shown to a room on the second highest floor, its décor not even registering before she threw herself, face down, on the quilt, and cried herself to sleep.

A loud and continuous noise woke her in the middle of the night. At first, she thought it was rain beating down. But, when she struggled off the bed and went over to where sliding glass doors led out onto a balcony, Megan discovered that it was wind. A strong, howling wind which was actually rocking the building.

A nervous phone call to Reception brought reassurance that there was no need for alarm, the hotel was rock-solid and built to withstand this kind of gale, which was not uncommon in the autumn months and would probably blow itself out in a day or two.

Till then, however, the helicopters would be grounded and guests could neither leave nor come to the island.

Megan felt sick at this news. She was quite desperate to get away as soon as possible so that she could get a prescription of the morning-after pill.

But then she had a second thought. 'You must have a doctor on the island,' she asked Reception.

'We do. But Dr Wilkinson had to go to the mainland yesterday to attend a wedding. He's due back first thing in the morning, but, with the wind and all, he might not make it. Are you ill, madam? Is there anything I can do to help?'

'No, no, I'm not ill. It can wait, I suppose.'

Now that she thought about it, she recalled her doctor saying she had seventy-two hours to take the morning-after pill. She'd been in a right panic at the time, frightened that she might weaken and let James make love to her. That was why she had decided in the end to go on the Pill. She didn't like the idea of the morning-after pill, but she liked the idea of falling pregnant to James—especially now—even less.

'Oh, God,' she said aloud as her head whirled.

'Can I get you something, madam?' the man on the line enquired kindly. 'A hot drink perhaps. Or a brandy.'

'A brandy would be lovely,' she agreed, and five minutes later she was sitting in an armchair by the wind-lashed window, sipping brandy and thinking that she only had herself to blame really. It had been wrong of her to let James think a baby was possible. She should have been honest with him about not being ready yet for a child.

But that was as far as her honesty could have taken her. If she'd told him she knew he didn't love her, then their marriage

would have been over anyway. For how could their relationship survive after that? It was a matter of losing respect. Him
for her, and her for him.

But James was wrong about her trying to hurt him.

She wasn't. She loved him. Perversely, her love for him
was stronger now than ever.

Tears slipped down her cheeks as she recalled his obvious
sincerity when he'd said he'd wanted to make a good life with
her, full of caring and commitment. Well, any chance of that
good life was gone now.

Another horrible thought slid into her mind. When she
finally got off this island, she would have to go home to her
parents, she supposed. Where else could she go? She didn't
have any friends. None who hadn't been James's friends first.
She didn't have a job, or any money of her own, her allow-
ance having been stopped when she married James.

The prospect of facing her mother was infinitely depressing. Not quite what she needed at that moment.

It took her quite some time to fall asleep again, but when
she woke to the morning light the wind had thankfully
stopped. By ten, Megan was on a helicopter flight to Cairns.
Shortly before three that afternoon, she was landing at Mascot
Airport in Sydney. It was cold and raining, the wretched
weather matching her mood. The taxi driver didn't speak to
her during the thankfully short drive to Bellevue Hill, for
which she was grateful.

The sight of the beautiful home she'd lived in with James
brought fresh grief. And fresh worries. Would he have already
rung Roberta, and told her what had happened? Would she
be greeted by a hostile housekeeper?

She hoped not. She could not bear much more.

CHAPTER THIRTEEN

ROBERTA answered the doorbell with shock on her face. Clearly James hadn't informed his housekeeper of what had happened, which was a relief.

'I thought you weren't due home till Tuesday,' Roberta said, looking and sounding puzzled. 'Where's the boss?'

Megan steeled herself for the woman's reaction.

'He's not with me. We've broken up, Roberta. I've come home by myself to pack and move out.'

The housekeeper looked even more shocked. 'But I thought... I mean... Oh, Megan, that's a real shame.'

'Yes,' Megan agreed, trying her best not to cry. But her chin was beginning to wobble. 'It is. But it was inevitable.' Megan carried her bag inside the cavernous foyer, dropping it onto the marble-tiled floor with a weary sigh.

'Why do you say that?' Roberta asked as she closed the door.

Megan scooped in a deep, gathering breath and turned round to face the housekeeper. 'Because he doesn't love me, Roberta.'

'What? Why, that's rubbish! He does so love you.'

'I'm sorry, Roberta, but you're mistaken. He never loved me. Right from the start. All he wanted was a wife and a child.'

'I don't believe that.'

Megan sighed. 'He admitted it, Roberta.'

The housekeeper's mouth fell open, then snapped shut. 'Well, I never!' Now she looked both shocked and affronted. 'Oh, you poor dear.'

Megan gave her a wan smile. 'Would you come upstairs and help me get packed up? I have quite a bit of stuff.' Not just her clothes but also her art equipment, plus all her paintings.

'You're going today?'

'James said he wanted me out of the house by the time he returned.'

'*What?* The bastard!'

Megan shook her head. 'No, Roberta, he's nothing of the kind. Not really. He's very upset with me. The thing is…I gave him the impression when I agreed to go on this second honeymoon that I was quite happy to try for another baby. But I wasn't. I was on the Pill and he found them.'

'Oh…'

'He was very, *very* angry with me.'

'Yes, I can imagine. But surely he can understand why you're afraid to get pregnant again this soon. You went through a lot when you lost your baby.'

'Yes. Yes, I did.' She almost told the housekeeper then that this was when she found out James didn't love her, but felt that was taking confidences too far. They weren't close friends, after all. And the woman would no doubt want to go on working for James. It was a well-paid position which included her husband. They would find it hard to find a better one.

'Maybe you can patch things up,' the housekeeper said.

'No, Roberta. It's over.'

The housekeeper frowned. 'I find it hard to believe Mr Logan doesn't love you. The way he acts…I could have sworn…' She seemed genuinely perplexed. 'Look, maybe he does, but doesn't realise it.'

'That's sweet of you to say, but I can't afford to think like that. I've got into the trouble I'm in by being a hopeless romantic. It's time I grew up and faced life as it is, and not as I'd like it to be.'

'So where are you going to go?' Roberta asked as both women trudged up the winding staircase.

'To my parents' place, I suppose. They live in Woolahra.'

'That's not too far away. I'll get Bill to drive you and your things over, if you like.'

'It's all right, I can drive myself.' She did have a small car, a twenty-first-birthday present that her parents had bought her. It was not as flashy as anything James drove but it got her around. Not that she'd driven anywhere since her miscarriage. She hadn't had the confidence.

'Are you sure, Megan?' Roberta asked doubtfully.

'Positive.'

It was getting on for six by the time Megan pulled into the driveway of her family home, which, whilst not a twenty-million-dollar mansion with a view to die for, was still a substantial two-storeyed house with wrap-around verandahs top and bottom and large, well-looked-after grounds. Even with the present property market slump, it was worth a heap, having been a wedding present from Megan's grandfather to his only son and heir.

The Donnelly family had emigrated to Australia from Ireland shortly after the first world war, Megan's paternal great-grandfather making a small fortune with an industrial patent for a new packaging machine. His son—Megan's grandfather—had increased his father's wealth with some wise investments in property in the inner suburbs of Sydney, including this house, bought back in the fifties for a song. Megan's own father—not such an astute businessman as it turned out—had succeeded in greatly reducing his inherited fortune when he decided to sell several of these properties and put the money into the stock market just before the eighties crash.

Megan had heard the story of his disastrous investments so many times over the years, she'd lost count. Her mother never let an opportunity go by to rub in her father's failures. Losing money was the worst possible sin in Janet Donnelly's eyes. Megan was well aware of the reception she would get after revealing she'd left her seriously wealthy husband of less than six months.

Fortunately, her mother had still not returned from her Saturday afternoon's bridge party when she arrived, giving Megan the chance to deposit all her things in her old room and gather herself for what was going to be an unpleasant reunion.

Her father, the dear man, fussed around her, making her tea and generally being sweet. She kept her explanation to him pretty simple but truthful, eliciting words of comfort and understanding. She wasn't hoping for more of the same when her mother came home.

Megan was back upstairs in her bedroom when that happened, Janet Donnelly's return heralded by voices coming up the stairs, the woman's loud and strident, the man's low and muffled.

Megan's mother burst into her room without knocking.

'Your father tells me you've left your husband,' were her first words, spoken with disapproval and disgust.

Megan was astounded to find that she wasn't instantly reduced to a panic attack, which she once might have been. Instead, she straightened her spine and gazed with surprisingly cool eyes at the woman who'd given birth to her.

'Actually, that's not quite accurate,' she replied calmly. 'I didn't leave James. He threw me out. Sent me back home from Dream Island with orders to be out of the house by the time he returned.'

Janet Donnelly looked totally floored. 'Good lord! Why on earth would he do such an appalling thing?'

'He found out I was on the Pill.'

'The Pill!' she practically screamed. 'You were on the Pill on your second honeymoon? Oh, you stupid, stupid girl!'

Megan had expected no less. Amazingly, the insults slid off her like water off a duck's back.

'But not all is lost yet,' her mother raved on, pacing round the room with her hands rubbing her cheeks as they did when she was agitated. 'He's just angry with you, that's all.'

Megan almost laughed. The word 'angry' did not quite describe James's mood at the time.

Her mother ground to a halt in front of her. 'You should not have left the house,' she said, shaking her index finger at her. 'You never voluntarily leave the marital home. Now, here is what you have to do. You go home straight away, and when James gets back you apologise profusely, and then you—'

'No,' Megan interrupted firmly. 'I won't be going back home, Mother. And I certainly won't be apologising. For anything. James doesn't love me. He never did. All he ever wanted from me was a child. He deliberately got me pregnant in the first place to make sure I was capable of having children, unlike his poor first wife, whom he divorced when he found out she was barren.'

'Really? That's not what I heard. I heard she refused to have children. But that's beside the point. Marriage has nothing to do with love in the long run, my girl. It's about security, and status. James Logan is a brilliant and very rich man. Marrying him was the wisest thing you ever did. Divorcing him would be crazy.'

'I don't want to be married to a man who doesn't love me,' Megan argued.

'Oh, for pity's sake!'

'Yes, for pity's sake,' came another voice. Male.

Megan's eyes widened as she watched her father—normally quelled into silence when his wife was having a hissy fit—stride confidently into the room and come to stand beside her.

'If you had any pity in you at all, Janet,' he addressed his wife as he wound a gentle arm around his daughter's somewhat stiff shoulders, 'you would be comforting your daughter, not haranguing her into returning to a man who doesn't love her. I, better than anyone, know what it's like to be married to someone who doesn't love and respect them. I wouldn't wish that fate on a dog, let alone my own daughter, whom, I might add, is in no way stupid. She is a fine and intelligent girl who deserves better than a ruthless liar of a husband. Deserves better, too, than a mother who thinks of nothing but money.'

Megan's mother had the decency to blush. But not for long. Soon her haughtily handsome face lost all shame, her dark eyes hardening once again.

'If Megan had had the wretchedly poor childhood I had, then she might appreciate money more. But what does she know of doing without? Why, she's never even had a job! And the same applies to you, Henry. You were born with a silver spoon in your mouth. Both of you went to the best of schools and had the best of educations. You didn't have to leave school when you were fourteen to work in a chicken-gutting factory. By the time I was twenty I would have done anything not to be poor.'

'Even marry a man you didn't love,' her husband accused.

Megan could see the confusion in her mother's face. 'But that's not true. I did love you, Henry. I thought you were the loveliest, nicest man and the best husband in the world. But then you lost all that money, and I...I was just so angry with you.' The tears which suddenly flooded her mother's eyes stunned Megan. She'd never seen her mother cry. Not once.

No, that wasn't true. She had seen her mother cry once. When her grandmother had died. Megan had been about twelve. Her mother had just come out of the mortuary, the day before the funeral. She'd climbed back into the car—Megan had been waiting outside for her. Her mother had just sat there behind the wheel, saying nothing for ages. Finally, she'd muttered something about how old her mother looked for a woman of only fifty-five. Old and defeated.

It was then that she'd started to cry, terribly noisy sobs which shook her shoulders. She'd dropped her head into her hands against the steering wheel and wept for ages. Megan had found her mother's tears disturbing at the time, not knowing what to say or do. It wasn't like her mother not to be in control.

This time, Megan knew what to do. She went forward and put her arms around her mother. 'It's all right, Mum,' she said. 'I know you love Father.'

Her mother's head jerked up, her eyes glistening. 'You called me Mum.'

Megan smiled. 'Do you mind?'

'No. No, I rather like it.'

'What about you, Dad? Can I call you that instead of Father?'

'Of course you can, dear girl.'

'You will still have to get yourself a lawyer, Megan,' her mother pointed out, quickly getting back to her usual priorities. 'Divorces can be messy.'

'I don't think this one will be,' Megan said. 'I don't want anything from James.'

'Don't want anything!' Her mother looked horrified. 'But...but he should be made to pay for what he did. I mean...it's not as though he can't afford it. He has millions and millions.'

'So have I,' her father said so quietly that Megan wasn't sure she'd heard right.

'What was that you said, Henry?' her mother asked, obviously not sure either.

'I said I have millions and millions as well. About two hundred and eighty million, at last count.'

They both stared at him. Megan knew her family was well off but not to that extent.

Her father smiled a smile unlike any she'd ever seen him smile before. It was close to being smug.

'When I lost all that money in the eighties crash, it was, really, only paper money that I'd lost. There seemed no point in selling any of the stocks and shares considering they were at rock-bottom, so I kept them. But I watched the market closely for signs of overheating, warning signs that I'd ignored in the eighties. I wasn't going to get caught a second time. I always resolved that if I regained all my losses and made a healthy profit by the year 2000, I would get out of the stock market and invest my money back in property. Which I did, avoiding the seven-eleven crash in 2001. I bought units, by the way, near the city. Then, after the 2001 crash, when I saw an opportunity to buy lots of blue-chip shares at greatly undervalued prices, I did, then rode the subsequent boom till early 2007, when I saw signs of overheating, and got out again. If you recall, the global financial crisis began soon after that. But I haven't been adversely affected. In fact, I've been making a lot more money, due to the sharp rise in rents.'

Megan could not help being impressed.

'Megan doesn't need any money from Logan,' he said proudly. 'I have more than enough to keep her. And even you, my love,' he added, giving his wife a somewhat sardonic glance.

'Henry Donnelly!' she pronounced with a huff and a puff. 'You are a wickedly deceitful man. But a very clever one,' she added, rushing forward to give him a big hug. 'Now we can buy a bigger house.'

'We won't be doing that, madam,' he refuted firmly. 'This house is way big enough. What we might do, however, is go on one of those world cruises, in our own luxury stateroom. And we could stop over in Paris, where I could buy you some seriously expensive clothes. Would you like that?'

'Oh, Henry,' she gushed, and fluttered her eyelashes up to him, solving the mystery for Megan of why her father had married her mother in the first place.

'Now, let's hear no more about Megan returning to that louse of a husband of hers.'

'He's not a louse,' Megan heard herself say before she could stop herself.

Both parents stared at her.

'You're not going to tell me that you still love that man,' her mother said, sounding very much like her old self again. 'Not after what he's done.'

Megan sighed. 'I'm afraid I do.'

'That's ridiculous!'

'Janet,' Henry warned. 'Leave her be. We can't always stop loving someone, just because they hurt us.'

Her mother heard the innuendo behind those words and shut up.

'I won't be underfoot for too long,' Megan said. 'I'm going to get myself a job. And then I'm going to move out. I don't want you to keep me, Father—oh, I mean Dad—but if you really want to help, then perhaps you have a unit somewhere near the city which I could rent from you. For a reduced price, that is.'

'No trouble, my dear. But what kind of a job do you think you could get? Unemployment is rather high in Sydney, don't forget. And you're hardly trained for much.'

'Nathan Price said last year he'd give me a job at his gallery. He said I had a good eye for exhibiting artwork.'

'That sounds splendid,' he said, nodding. 'And now, madam,' he went on, turning to his wife, 'what's for dinner?'

'I thought we might go out to eat, darling,' she returned sweetly. 'After all, we can well afford it.'

'I don't think Megan's in the mood for going out.'

'Don't worry about me,' Megan said quickly. 'You two go out, by all means. I'll make myself some toast.'

'See, Henry? She'll be fine,' she heard her mother say as she steered her husband out of the door.

Megan sank down on the side of her bed when they left, thinking to herself that, surprisingly, she just might be fine. Not happy, mind. But she would survive. She'd grown up a lot during this past week. Grown in confidence, and courage. The Megan who'd lost her baby had been incapable of facing the truth, or in taking action because of that truth. Yesterday, she'd done more than that. She'd not just faced the truth, but she'd also spoken it out loud, despite knowing the consequences.

But now she had to live with those consequences. Had to live her life without the man she loved.

Thinking of James brought an inevitable jab of pain. But no tears. She'd cried enough last night, then again on the plane back to Sydney. The time for tears was over, but not, it seemed, for memories. Of this last week. Megan did not totally regret going on their second honeymoon. How could she? The sex had been incredible. And James's passion had been real. If nothing else, she *had* made him mad with lust for her. It wasn't love, she supposed. But it was something.

As she sat here, remembering, she wondered what James was doing. Had he left Dream Island yet? Or was he going to stay there till Tuesday?

She couldn't imagine him staying. He would come back before then. He might even already be on his way home.

Home…

Megan glanced around the room which had been her sanctuary during her growing-up years. It was a large room, with a window that overlooked the back garden, and a window seat where she'd spent countless hours sketching. It wasn't painted pink, as some girls' rooms were. It was a pale olive-green, with cream trim. The bed was a double, with a colourful patchwork quilt. Her furniture was made in pine, varnished so as not to stain or scratch easily. Besides the bed, there were two bedside tables, a dressing table and a bookcase—filled with books on art. An empty easel stood in one corner.

She'd never covered her walls with posters as some teenagers did. Above her bed hung a print of Monet's 'Waterlilies'. She didn't have an *en suite* bathroom. The main bathroom was next door. But she did have a walk-in wardrobe, which at that moment was bulging with all the things she'd brought home with her. Not just clothes, but also her artwork.

At least she still had her first love, she thought. She wasn't sure if she could survive if she didn't have that.

Breathing in deeply, Megan stood up and walked over to pull out the two paintings she'd done since her miscarriage. Carefully, she positioned the canvasses side by side on the easel—they weren't big paintings—then walked back to sit on the end of the bed and look them over with a fresh and more critical eye.

They were both self-portraits, although you couldn't really tell it was her. The paintings were impressionistic in style, with the woman's facial features not well-defined. They were both nudes, painted in black and white. And they were good, she decided. She'd show them to Nathan tomorrow, when she went to ask him for a job. She had a feeling he was going to like them.

James might have, too, if he'd ever seen them. Not that he'd ever been seriously interested in her art. He'd pretended to be for a while but that was when he'd been seducing her.

For a split second Megan felt a spurt of bitterness. But she quickly let it go. Bitterness was a self-destructive emotion. She would not entertain it. James had valid excuses for doing what he did. She could see that now. He was a damaged soul, incapable of true love. Incapable of understanding other people's feelings.

Empathy was not his strong point.

Which was really sad. Couldn't he see that his behaviour

was just as cruel and insensitive as his own father's? He had a lot to learn, if he thought he'd make a good father. One hell of a lot.

Megan's heart suddenly raced as she thought of the morning-after pill which the doctor had given her before she left Dream Island and which she hadn't yet been able to bring herself to take.

Not because she wanted to have a baby at this stage. She didn't. But if by some incredibly bad stroke of luck she had conceived, did she have the right to stop that child from being born? On the other side of the coin, hadn't she just concluded James was not the wonderful father material she'd once thought he would be?

It was becoming clear to her that he had all the wrong motives in wanting a child so desperately. Megan believed now it was a male-ego thing, a desire to prove to his own rotten father that he could do a lot better at parenting than he did.

But how could James be a good father to their child, when he didn't love his child's mother? What example was that?

Love was what made a good parent. And a good family.

Think, Megan, a voice piped up in her head. You're not going back to James. If you have his child, he'll fight you for it. You know he will. Don't take the risk. Do something now whilst you've got the chance.

Megan rose and walked over to where she'd left her handbag on the desk. Opening it, she retrieved the tablet and carried it with her out of her bedroom to the bathroom next door. There, she looked for a glass to fill with water.

There wasn't one.

She popped the tablet in her mouth, turned on the tap and cupped her hands under the stream of water.

Such a simple thing to swallow a tablet. But she just couldn't do it. In the end, she spat the tablet down the toilet and flushed it away.

She would let fate decide. Or was it God? Whatever, she would live with the consequences of her actions. And if there was a baby, she would not let James take it away from her. She would fight for her child. And love it, no matter what.

CHAPTER FOURTEEN

AT THE precise moment Megan flushed the morning-after pill down the toilet, James woke from the drugged sleep which had kept him in la-la land that entire Sunday. He'd finally found some painkillers the night before—in a first-aid kit in a kitchen drawer—long after the wind had started howling, the sound driving him almost as insane as the pain screaming in his head. He'd swallowed double the recommended dose of a well-known calmative analgesic and eventually passed out.

The sound of his cellphone ringing elicited a groan. As he rolled over, his fumbling fingers knocked the damned thing onto the floor. He practically fell out of the bed picking it up, resolving then and there never to take more than the recommended dose of any medication ever again.

'James Logan,' he muttered blearily into the phone.

'Wow,' a man's voice said. 'Is that a hangover I'm hearing? You can't possibly have been asleep. It's not even seven yet. A bit early for bed. Unless…whoops, have I rung at a bad time?'

James flopped back onto the bed with a weary sigh. It was Russell. 'Any time would be a bad time at the moment,' he said bleakly.

'Sorry, mate. Didn't mean to interrupt anything. If you like, I could ring back at another time.'

'No, no. That's not what I meant. Look, you might as well know what's happened.'

'Er—that doesn't sound too good.'

'It isn't.'

'Tell me.'

'Megan's not here. She's gone home.'

'What? But why?'

'I asked her to leave.' Hell, now, wasn't that an understatement? James grimaced when he thought of how irrational he'd been yesterday. But he'd been blind with rage. Though not so blind once the reality of the situation became clear. Megan didn't love him. She hated him. Of course she did. Any woman would.

But that didn't give her the right to do what she'd done. He might have been rather brutal in his condemnation of her actions, but he hadn't been totally wrong. Had he?

'Why on earth would you do a stupid thing like that?' Russell demanded to know.

'The bottom line is, mate, that Megan knows. About how and why I married her. She overheard you and Hugh discussing the subject when she was in hospital after losing the baby. She said you thought she was asleep.'

'Geez, James. I'm sorry. We did think she was asleep.'

'It's all right, Russ. It's not your fault. The fault is all mine.'

'But if she's known the truth for this long, why didn't she say something before now? I mean…why tell you when you were on a second honeymoon?'

'She didn't. It all came out when I accidentally found out she was on the Pill. I went off my brain, as you can imagine. She'd led me to believe we were trying for another baby when, in fact, all she wanted was revenge before she told me to get lost.'

'Revenge? What kind of revenge?'

'It's hard to explain.'

'Try.'

'Looking back, I think she was trying to get me to fall in love with her. Or at least in lust with her. She acted differently. And she dressed differently. She was very...provocative.'

'Hot, you mean.'

'Yeah, hot. She had me going before we even got here. And she kept me going, believe me. I haven't felt that continuously horny since I was at uni.'

'Not even with Jackie? You had the hots for her all right.'

'True. But this was somehow different. Like I said, it's hard to explain. She told me on the plane that Megan the mouse was gone and that she had a new image. How ironic was that? A new image. The penny should have dropped at that point. I mean, the girl I married was nothing like the girl I took away with me to Dream Island. I should have known something was up. The trouble was, I was too busy thinking about what was up of mine!'

'Er—I wouldn't blame Megan entirely for her new image. I think that was partly Nicole's fault. She told me she encouraged Megan to dress more sexily.'

'Whatever. The end result was the same. Megan got what she wanted. Me, madly in love with her.'

'What? I thought you were still hung up on Jackie?'

'Hell no. I can't stand that self-centred cow.'

'But you did meet up with her when you were overseas, didn't you? Just before your wedding to Megan.'

'I ran into her one day in New York, that's all. We only exchanged a few words.'

'Nothing else?'

'Bloody hell, Russ, you don't think I slept with her, do you?'

'I did wonder.'

James shook his head. 'What must you think of me?' he said wearily.

'I thought you were still in love with her. You never said you weren't.'

'Yeah, well, I'm saying so now.'

'That's good. Because that's the reason I'm ringing you. Jackie's been trying to get into contact with you. Your office told her that you'd be back from holiday on Tuesday and were sure to be at work first thing Wednesday morning. I only know this because your secretary rang to ask me if she did the right thing in not telling your ex where you were. Apparently Jackie said it was an emergency. Anyway, she said she could wait till Wednesday and made an appointment to see you around lunch-time. I didn't want you coming back without being prepared. Still, I suppose it won't matter much now that you and Megan have split up.'

'If you think I'd take Jackie back, you need your head read.'

'It's not *my* head which needs reading, mate. It's yours. You had the best girl in the world this time and you blew it. You should have told her the truth from the start, then you might have stood a chance.'

'I doubt it,' James muttered. 'Do you have any idea what Jackie might want?'

'What do women like that usually want? Money, I suppose.'

'Well, she won't be getting any.'

'What about Megan? You'll have to look after her, you know, or you'll have Hugh and me to answer to, not to mention Nicole. Don't make her go to some sleazebag divorce lawyer. Give her what she rightfully deserves, which is one hell of a lot.'

James thought of all the ugly things he'd said to her, and the ugly way he'd asked her to leave both the island and the house back in Sydney. He could still remember the look on her face. Had it been shock, or hurt? Whatever, she hadn't argued with him in the end. She'd just gone.

Maybe she shouldn't have done what she had, but he'd been the first offender. And the worst. If she'd wanted some revenge, who could blame her?

'Don't worry,' he said bleakly. 'I'll make sure she's looked after.' What would he need his money for now anyway? Having a family in the near future seemed highly unlikely. He wouldn't get over this in a hurry.

'So when are you coming back? If Megan's not there, you might as well get on a plane tomorrow.'

'Might as well.'

'Why don't you come over for dinner tomorrow night? I dare say you'll need some company by then.'

'Are you sure Nicole will want me there? I have a feeling I might not be her favourite person, especially after you tell her what's happened.'

'Don't be ridiculous.'

James didn't think it was at all ridiculous. He'd always known Nicole didn't care for him the way she did Hugh. And he could see why. He wasn't a very likeable person. He was arrogant and selfish. And as insensitive as Megan had said he was.

'OK,' he said, sighing. 'See you tomorrow night, then. Seven do?'

'Seven will be fine. And bring a bottle. Or two. You can sleep the night.'

'Will do. And thanks, Russ.'

'For what?'

'For always being there for me. You and Hugh. I don't know what I'd do without you.'

There was a short, sharp silence followed by a wry laugh. 'Watch it, buddy. You're getting sentimental in your old age.'

'I guess that's what truly falling in love does for you,' he said, and hung up.

Russell slowly replaced the phone then stood up and went in search of Nicole. She was in the kitchen, preparing dinner.

'I rang James about Jackie wanting to contact him,' he said, hoisting himself up onto one of the kitchen stools.

Nicole looked up, a frown on her lovely face. 'I wish you hadn't.'

'I almost wish I hadn't, too. Then I wouldn't know what I know now.'

Nicole's frown deepened. 'Which is?'

'It's over. James's marriage to Megan.'

'No!'

'I'm afraid so.'

'What happened?'

Russell told her everything that James had told him.

'What utter rubbish!' Nicole exclaimed once he'd finished. 'Megan doesn't have a vengeful bone in her body. The man's a fool as well as a right royal bastard!'

Russell sighed. James was right. Nicole didn't overly like him.

'I don't think you can blame James entirely for what happened, or for what he thinks. Megan did lie to him. She made him believe they were trying for another baby when she was on the Pill. On top of that, she dressed and acted like some sexpot all the time.'

Nicole grimaced. 'I suppose I'm to blame for some of that.'

'I did point that out to him,' Russell said drily.

'I was only trying to get James to fall for her!'

'Well, you succeeded. The poor devil's even more cut up about this than he was about Jackie.'

'He really loves her now?' Nicole questioned him. 'Are you sure? This is James we're talking about here, not you or Hugh. He might just be saying that he does.'

'Why, in God's name, would he do that? It's not as though he's going after her. He says she hates him and that there's no point. You should have heard him, Nicole. He's totally shattered.'

'I find that hard to believe.'

'You'll see for yourself tomorrow night. I've invited him for dinner.'

'Oh, no, you didn't!'

'Have some compassion, darling. He's hurting terribly.'

Nicole sighed. 'Oh, all right. But I'll bet poor Megan is hurting more. I wonder if she's already moved out of the house.'

'I couldn't say. But I would imagine so. She wouldn't want to be there when James got home, from the sounds of things.'

'Where would she go, do you think? She doesn't exactly have loads of friends.'

Russell shrugged. 'Her parents' place, I suppose.'

Nicole winced. 'Poor Megan. Blind Freddie could see that mother of hers was cock-a-hoop when she married James. She's not going to be too popular, leaving her super-dooper meal-ticket. I think I might give Kara a call, find out Mr and Mrs Donnelly's phone number and address. Her mother was a friend of Mrs Donnelly. Played bridge with her, or something like that.'

Russell gave his wife a pained look. 'Do you really think you should get involved, Nicole?'

'Russell McClain, I have to tolerate your inviting James here for dinner because you're his friend. Well, I count myself a friend of Megan's. What kind of friend would I be if I didn't see how she was, or offer my help?'

'As long as that's all you're going to do. I don't want her living here or anything like that.'

'Please don't tell me what to do or not to do, Russell,' she said sternly. 'I'm your partner, not your employee.'

'Yes, dear.'

'That's better.' And she returned to cutting up the vegetables.

Russell rolled his eyes once her back was turned. Why was

it that women couldn't do what men did when a relationship was over—get drunk and leave things be? But no, they had to meddle. Anyone with half a brain could see that James's marriage was dead in the water. Nothing short of a miracle was going to put it right. But he supposed she had to try. That was what made Nicole the wonderful person she was. He really loved her generosity of spirit and her empathy for others.

Sometimes, however, she was just too kind for her own good!

CHAPTER FIFTEEN

WHEN Megan woke the next morning, for a split second she didn't remember where she was. But then, as she glanced around her old bedroom with clearing eyes and mind, the memories flooded in, and so did the despair.

She moaned and rolled over, burying her face into the pillows.

I can't bear it. Any of it. Not any more. It's too much.

Jamming curled fists into her mouth to stop herself from sobbing out loud, she scrunched her body up into a foetal ball and willed herself back to sleep, where at least there was some kind of peace. It took a long time, but she finally achieved her objective.

She was still there, dead to the world, when Nicole rang to speak to her, Megan startled back to abrupt consciousness when her mother shook her shoulder.

'What?' she exclaimed, sitting bolt upright.

'There's someone on the phone for you,' Janet Donnelly said softly, her hand covering the mouthpiece of the mobile receiver she was holding. 'Nicole McClain.'

Megan blinked. How on earth did Nicole know she was here?

There was only one answer to that question: James must have rung Russell and told him what had happened. Then

Nicole must have concluded that Megan had nowhere to go but back to her parents' place.

This last thought brought bucketloads of dismay.

Megan didn't want to talk to Nicole. She didn't want to talk to anyone. But how could she refuse with her mother standing there? Janet Donnelly was a stickler for manners.

'Thank you.' She took the phone, waiting till her mother had left the room before she spoke.

'Hello,' she said.

'Megan. It's Nicole.'

'Yes. Mum said it was you.'

'You sound dreadful.'

'Do I?' She'd thought she sounded normal.

'Yes, you poor thing. Look, I know what happened. Russell had to ring James yesterday over an urgent business matter and James told him. I have to say that I think he's acted like an absolute bastard. Now that Russell can't hear me, I can say that.'

Megan sighed. 'He wasn't entirely to blame, Nicole.'

'Rubbish. He was totally to blame. He should never have married you in the first place. It was wicked of him.'

'I suppose so.'

'You sound so defeated. Oh, this is dreadful. So tell me, what are you going to do? Not long-term. *Today*. What are you going to do today?'

A strange little laugh escaped Megan's throat. 'I was going to get up first thing this morning and get myself a job, down at an art gallery I know well. The owner said he'd give me one any time. But I find I don't have the energy, or the will power. I just want to pull the blanket back over my head and sleep forever.'

'That's depression. But you mustn't do that. Look, Monday's my day off. I'm going to come and get you and we'll go down to that art gallery together. Where is it, by the way?'

'Bondi.'

'Perfect. We'll do lunch afterwards. I know just the place. Now, what time is it? Umm…ten-seventeen. I'll give you till eleven to be ready. No longer, mind. Get up straight away and get yourself into a hot shower. Put on something bright. If you want a job in an art gallery you need some pizzazz.'

Megan didn't know what to say. Not no, that was for sure. Nicole was like some whirlwind. But a nice one. Her sympathy and kindness were much appreciated, but they opened the floodgates.

'Thank you,' she choked out at last.

'My pleasure. Now, hop to it and no more tears.'

'How did you know I was crying?'

'Megan, I'm a woman too.'

And an incredibly beautiful one, Megan was reminded when she opened the front door right on eleven.

Dressed in a chic black suit with an open-necked white silk blouse underneath, Nicole looked like the kind of woman who just might break that glass ceiling people were always talking about. She looked not just beautiful but also sophisticated and intelligent and, yes, in total command of herself and everything around her.

Megan envied her obvious confidence, though not her looks. If there was one positive leftover from this last week, it was that she'd come to believe she was a very attractive girl in her own right, with a good figure and some style of her own. When James had first picked out the yellow woollen dress she was wearing today, she'd felt it was too bright, and refused to wear it. Now neither its colour nor its form-fitting style bothered her one bit.

'Now, *that*,' Nicole said, looking Megan up and down, 'is just the ticket. Come on, kiddo, get your handbag and we're off.'

'I have a couple of paintings I want to take with me,' Megan said, and pointed to the sheet-wrapped bundle in the hallway near by. 'If you carry my handbag for me, I'll carry them.'

'Yours?' Nicole asked on their way down the front steps.

'Yes. I want to see what Nathan thinks of them.'

'And Nathan is?'

'The owner of the gallery. Nathan Price.'

'Don't know him. But that's all right. I don't know much about art at the best of times. Are they any good?'

'*I* think so.'

Nicole beamed over at her. 'I like the sound of that. Very positive.'

'It's hard not to be positive around you, Nicole.'

'What a lovely thing to say!'

And what a lovely person you are, Megan thought during the drive to the art gallery. No wonder Russell loves you.

This last thought, however, was a double-edged sword, because it led to her wishing for the moon again. What she would not give to have had James look at her the way Russell always looked at Nicole, and Hugh at Kathryn. But he never had. And he never would now.

Nicole fell silent behind the wheel, not sure whether she should bring up the subject of how Megan felt about James at this early stage. She had no intention of telling her that James believed he'd fallen in love with *her* during their second honeymoon, because quite frankly she didn't believe any such thing. Fallen into lust, probably, with the more sexy-looking Megan. Nicole had little faith in James's version of being in love, since he was supposed to have been madly in love with that pathetic, up-herself supermodel who was all sex and no substance.

Nicole would wait till she saw James tonight before she made any judgement on that score. She was becoming quite good at reading body language, her job in real estate making her much more astute in that regard. She knew straight away these days if a client was a serious buyer, or just a time waster. James would have trouble deceiving her in the flesh.

Meanwhile, she needed to find out how Megan felt about her husband. Obviously, she was very hurt. Maybe she even thought she hated him. But hate was often the other side of love.

But probing Megan's obviously fragile emotions could wait till lunch-time. She'd buy Megan a glass of wine or two, and see if that would relax her enough for Nicole to broach such a delicate subject.

'Whereabouts is this art gallery?' she asked as they approached Bondi.

'Turn left at the next set of lights. And then take the second street on the right. The gallery's about two hundred metres down that road, next to a small row of shops. There's parking behind it, so that's not a worry. Not that there would be much trouble parking on a Monday.'

Nicole found the gallery, a pale grey, cement-rendered two-storeyed building with an alleyway next to it which led from the small car park at the back to the front, where a huge picture window gave any passer-by a good look of the artwork beyond. One glance showed that they didn't just exhibit paintings. There was a large display of vibrantly coloured pottery pieces not far from the window. Very interesting, it was. But not to Nicole's taste. She embraced simplicity these days, her home not filled with what she thought of as useless ornaments and knick-knacks. Her once extensive and very expensive wardrobe had also been reduced to basics, nothing but jeans and casual gear, plus a selection of classically tailored power suits bought off the rack. No more overpriced designer fashions for her. And no more frivolous party frocks, either!

A tinkling bell rang as one pushed open the gallery's front door, a blond-headed man in a pink shirt and paisley tie immediately appearing from a back room. For a moment he didn't seem to recognise Megan. But then he came forward with a camp smile broadening his thin, aesthetically handsome face.

'Megan, darling. Long time no see. My, don't you look scrumptious? And what do you have for me? Some new paintings at last? Do give me a look-see.'

Nicole appreciated that he totally ignored her to concentrate on Megan, and possibly business. There again, she thought ruefully, gay men did tend to ignore her. When a gay guy came in to buy a house, she always directed him to one of the other salespeople. Usually Derek, who wasn't gay, but could have been by the looks of him.

'They're different from what I used to do,' Megan said as she laid the paintings down on a counter top and began unwrapping the sheet. Once the sheet was undone, she carried the two paintings over to a long sideboard and leant them up against the wall. 'They have to be looked at from a bit of a distance,' Megan said, then stepped away from them.

Both Nathan Price and Nicole were momentarily struck dumb. They weren't just good, Nicole thought. They were tours de force.

'Oh, my!' Nathan said, clasping both his cheeks in what could only be described as a camp gesture. But much better than words.

'You like them?' Megan enquired, her cheeks developing splotches of pink. As well they might.

Both were nudes. The first painting was entitled *Despair*. A very apt word. A brunette was sitting on a stool, with her shoulders slumped forward and her head in her hands. You couldn't see her face. Fortunately, this made her unrecognisable. Fortunately also, perhaps, you couldn't see anything too private. Even her nipples were obscured by bits of arms.

The second painting was not quite as discreet in that regard. This time the brunette was sitting astride a chair that was turned around, her bare arms resting along the top of the chair back. Fortunately, there was a solid middle panel to the back which stopped the painting from being pornographic, but she could see most of the subject's breasts, along with their very erect nipples.

Once again, however, Megan had contrived to make the subject unrecognisable as a self-portrait, with a clever use of hair and shadow falling across the brunette's face. Only one eye was clear, one incredible eye that held an expression which was as powerful as it was unmistakable.

The title of *Desire* was quite unnecessary.

It was the most erotically charged picture Nicole had ever seen.

'Has James seen these?' Nicole asked, her voice low and a little husky. But, dear heaven, looking at that painting had quickened her breathing. What it would do to a heterosexual male, she could only imagine.

'No,' Megan admitted.

Nicole wasn't surprised.

'I could get thirty grand for that painting alone,' Nathan pronounced, jabbing a heavily beringed finger towards the one entitled *Desire*. 'I have several wealthy clients who buy nudes. Not quite so much for the other one. Maybe only twenty.'

Megan just stared at him. My God. Fifty thousand dollars! She'd thought they were good, but this was breathtaking news!

'Of course, if you do a few more,' Nathan added, his eyes alight with artistic fervour, 'you could have an exhibition. If we time it right—say, just before Christmas—and do some proper marketing, then the sky's the limit.'

Megan didn't know what to say.

'You've found your forte, darling,' Nathan gushed. 'Good nudes always sell. But might I suggest that you do a blonde next time? And change your setting. Your friend here,' he said, giving Nicole a highly objective once-over, 'now, she'd make a good subject. But keep to the black and white theme. That's very effective.'

'What about a man?' Megan enquired, her mind filling with images of James in the buff. She didn't need him to sit for her. She could remember every line of his body. Every muscle.

'Even better,' Nathan enthused. 'You'd widen your market considerably with a few male nudes.'

Nicole just managed not to make a sound. But *really*!

'I wasn't talking about a few,' Megan said. 'Just one. It took me nearly three months to do those two.'

'Yes, but now that you know they're good,' Nathan pointed out smugly, 'you'll paint more quickly. Nothing like confidence to speed up the brushes, and the inspiration. It's over seven months till Christmas. If you do four more, that should be enough. Say two blondes and two men. How about that?'

'I don't know, Nathan. I really just came down here to get your opinion, and to ask you for a job.'

'A job! Why would James Logan's wife want a job?'

Megan hesitated, then decided there was no point in lying. 'We've split up.'

'So soon? Oh, dear heart, I'm so sorry. Sorry, too, that I can't offer you a job. But times are very tough at the moment. I man this place all by myself during the week. I do have a girl who comes in to help at the weekends and on exhibition nights but I can't really sack her just to hire you, can I?'

'Of course not.'

'Look, sweetie,' he said, walking forward to take her hands in his, 'use this opportunity to paint. Pour all the emotion which has to be seething inside you at the moment into your work.'

'I don't know, Nathan…' Megan's emotions weren't seething so much as sinking. She suddenly felt terribly tired again. 'I…I'll think about it.'

'Don't take them with you,' Nathan objected when she went to pick her paintings up again. 'What say I frame them and put them up on the wall straight away? See if we get any offers.'

'All right,' she said. 'But don't actually sell them without consulting me first. I'll give you my phone number.'

'It's a deal.'

'Are you sure you want to sell those paintings?' Nicole asked Megan over their pre-lunch drinks. Hers was a mineral water, whilst Megan's was a very nice Chardonnay from the Hunter Valley. They were in a local café. Nothing flash, but Nicole had been there before and the food was good. 'They're brilliant, but anyone who knows you will realise the brunette is you.'

'Is it that obvious?'

'Yes.'

Megan put down her glass of wine. 'What does it really matter?' she said. 'What does anything matter any more? It's not as though James will care. He doesn't care about me, or my paintings.'

'Are you quite sure about that?'

'Quite sure.'

'And do you still care about him, Megan?'

Megan looked away, and shook her head. 'I shouldn't. I know I shouldn't.'

'But you do.'

She nodded, no longer able to speak.

Nicole wasn't sure what to do, or what to say. All she knew was she had to make sure that what Megan believed was really the truth. If James didn't love her, then he could go stew in his own pathetic juice. But if he did really love her now, then, by God, he was going to know that this lovely girl still loved him back.

Nicole had come very close to losing Russell because of actions and words which could have been easily misinterpreted. Fortunately, the strength of their love for each other had won the day. But it had been a close call.

'James is coming to our place for dinner tonight,' she said.

Megan jerked her head back round to stare at Nicole, her eyes wide with surprise.

And reproach.

'It wasn't my idea,' Nicole hastily added. 'My better half thought James might need tea and sympathy. I couldn't really say no.'

Megan sighed resignedly. 'They're as thick as thieves, those two,' she said. 'Not to mention Hugh as well. Neither of them approved of James marrying me. But they stood by him on our wedding day and didn't say a word.'

'They wouldn't. They're very loyal to each other.'

'I don't understand it. They have nothing in common, except perhaps golf, and money. Why are they such good friends?'

'Russell didn't always have money,' Nicole pointed out. 'Besides, having things in common doesn't always make for a good friendship. They appreciate each other's qualities. And they understand each other. They know what makes each other tick and why they do what they do. They were at boarding school together. Shared a room. At uni, too. Till Russell's dad committed suicide. You do know about that, don't you?'

'Yes. Yes, James told me the whole sorry story after the to-do at your wedding.'

'It screwed Russell up for a long time. He became a right ruthless devil. But both James and Hugh stayed his friend.'

Megan frowned. 'Did you know that James's father was an abusive pig of a man?'

'Heavens, no. I had no idea. I don't think Russell knows that, either. If he does, he's never mentioned it.'

'James doesn't like to talk about it.'

'But he told you.'

'Only recently.'

During their second honeymoon, Nicole realised. When James said he fell in love with her...

Nicole thought about that all during their lunch together. And during the drive back to Woolahra.

'Thanks for the lunch, Nicole,' Megan said when they pulled up outside her parents' place. 'And for going to Nathan's with me.'

'So what are you going to do if he rings you and says he has a buyer for your paintings? Sell, or wait for an exhibition?'

'I'm not sure now. About either of those alternatives. They're very private paintings, Nicole. I never really thought about selling them. I just wanted to see if Nathan thought they were any good.'

'You don't have to sell them if you don't want to.'

'No. No, I don't.' She didn't like the idea of people she knew looking at them and knowing it was her. Well...sort of. She hadn't exactly posed that way. They were partly works of her imagination. But the emotions had been all hers. She sighed, then glanced over at Nicole. 'Are you going to tell James you were with me today?'

'Yes. Why not? You're my friend. He's not.'

'Really and truly, Nicole?'

Her vulnerability was just too touching for words. I'm going to kill that man if he doesn't really love you, Nicole thought as she bent over and gave Megan a kiss on the cheek. 'Of course you are. I'll call you some time tomorrow. Make sure you're putting your shoulder to the wheel, or whatever that saying is. Even if you decide not to sell those two particular paintings, that doesn't stop you from painting more. No slacking, now. And no sleeping in. The art world awaits its newest genius.'

'I wish,' Megan said with a wry laugh as she climbed out of the car.

'Wishes are made to be granted!' Nicole called after her.

Only some, Nicole, Megan though sadly as she waved goodbye. *Only some.*

CHAPTER SIXTEEN

I WOULD have been better off staying home, James thought grimly within minutes of his arrival at Russell's house. Roberta might have given him the cold shoulder ever since he'd arrived home earlier that afternoon. But he could withstand his housekeeper's chilly manner far better than Nicole's probing gaze. Mostly because he could escape it.

Tonight, he had no option but to tolerate being stared at, and not so subtly quizzed over what had *really* happened on Dream Island.

His patience wore thin very quickly.

'Sorry, chaps,' he said when he was still on his first glass of red. 'It was very kind of you to invite me here tonight but fact is, I'm not in the mood for conversation, or food. So I think I'd better go home.' It wasn't far from the house Russell had bought at Bondi to his own place in Bellevue Hill.

'Don't be silly,' Russell protested immediately. 'Look, we won't give you the third degree any more, will we, Nicole? Promise. But don't go. Have another drink.' And he poured some more wine into James's glass.

James sighed. 'I don't think you understand, Russ.'

'I think I do,' Nicole said, her green eyes turning soft and warm for the first time that evening. 'You really do love Megan, don't you?'

'More than I would ever have thought possible.'

'Then you're right,' she said. 'You shouldn't stay here tonight. You should get over to her parents' place pronto, and tell her so.'

'*What?* Good God, Nicole, what would be the point of that? Megan hates me.'

'No, James. She doesn't hate you. I had lunch with Megan today and she doesn't hate you at all. Just the opposite, in fact.'

His heart began pounding in his chest so hard and loud that its beat echoed in his ears. 'She still loves me?'

'Yes.'

'But how could she, after what I did?'

'Because she's Megan, that's why. She's good and kind and gentle. And very forgiving. She doesn't do revenge, James. Ever. Neither is she a deceiving cow. The only reason she would have been on that pill was because she just couldn't face having another baby this soon. It's only been three months, after all. She was probably just too scared to tell you. You can be rather intimidating, James, especially to someone like Megan.'

James stared at her for a long moment, then shook his head. 'If what you're saying is true, then she couldn't possibly still love me. Not now. Not after the way I've acted.'

'Love doesn't stop that easily, James. Not true love.'

James groaned. 'But she won't believe me if I tell her I love her! She'll think it's just another lie.'

Nicole shrugged. 'Then you'll have to convince her that it isn't, won't you? After all, what have you got to lose?'

James turned towards Russell, seeking the male opinion. Women sometimes could be a little too optimistic when it came to romantic matters. 'Russ, what do you think? Do you think I've got a chance?'

'Never known you to lose an argument, buddy. Or back away from a challenge. If you really, truly love Megan the way I love Nicole, then nothing short of death should stop you trying to win her back.'

'My God, you're right!' James said, bursting up from his chair, almost tipping it backwards.

'I take it you won't be staying for dinner, then,' Russell said drily.

James was already heading for the door. 'Sorry, mate,' he called back over his shoulder. 'Have to take a rain check on that.'

'Do you think I should have told him about those paintings as well?' Nicole asked after the door slammed shut.

Russell gave his wife a droll look. 'I think you've been enough of a blabbermouth for one night, don't you?'

Nicole coloured. 'I had to do *something*. He looked so sad, Russ. Sad and defeated. I've never seen James like that before.'

'He's never been in love before.'

'You said once that he was madly in love with Jackie Foster.'

'Nah. That was just lust, I reckon.' All of a sudden Russell thought of Jackie's appointment to see James this Wednesday. He hoped she wasn't going to cause any trouble.

Nicole immediately pounced. 'What is it?'

Russell considered telling Nicole, then decided against it. 'Nothing. Just hoping things turn out for James and Megan, that's all.'

James drove straight to Woolahra, the fire in his belly dampening a little by the time he turned down the tree-lined avenue where the Donnellys lived. He pulled into the kerb outside their front gate and glanced somewhat nervously outside their house.

Even if Megan did still love him—something he was beginning to doubt—he would not get a good reception from either her or her parents.

A glance in the rear-view mirror showed bloodshot eyes

and a two-day growth of beard. He hadn't had the energy to shave today after hardly sleeping last night. Thankfully, his clothes were neat and clean. Clenching his teeth down hard in his jaw, he climbed out of his car and made his way towards the front door. The lights were on upstairs, he'd noticed, so someone was home.

The doorbell echoed loudly in the house, but no footsteps came. He rang again. This time, he heard someone coming.

The door swung open and there she was. His Megan, looking stunning in a bright yellow dress which he recalled buying with her but which she'd never worn. Her hair was up in a stylish French roll, pearl drops in her ears. Her make-up was subtle, but superb, her very kissable lips outlined in gloss. Unlike a lot of men, James was extremely observant about the details of a woman's appearance.

She didn't say a single word for ages. Just stared at him.

Her lack of instant insults was encouraging, James thought.

Man, but he needed all the encouragement in the world at that moment. Never before had he felt so unsure of himself.

'I need to talk to you, Megan,' he said at last. 'Can I come in?'

Alarm zoomed into her big brown eyes. 'My parents aren't home,' she blurted out.

James frowned. What an odd thing to say. She sounded—and looked—almost frightened of him. Surely she didn't imagine he'd do anything violent, did she? He would never do her any harm. Never!

Megan tried to calm herself, but it was impossible. She could not believe that James was on her doorstep. Could not believe the irrational joy which had immediately fizzed through her body at the sight of him.

She'd been upstairs, trying to work up the enthusiasm to do what Nathan had said—paint some more nudes. But had found, astonishingly so, she didn't want to. Those two paintings had been one-offs, she'd come to realise, an artistic expression of her emotional torment at the time. They were also *extremely* private. She'd just decided to ring Nathan in the morning and withdraw them from sale when the front doorbell had rung. And now the source of all her past torment was standing there, wanting to talk to her. The same man who'd refused to let her talk to him, to explain. The same man who'd ordered her off the island, and out of his home, not to mention his life.

One look at his grimly determined face told her that he'd come to get her back. It was frightening that this thought thrilled her so much.

My God, don't you ever learn? He's probably worked out that you might have fallen pregnant without your pills. He's a smart man. Very smart.

A good dose of indignant outrage masked the desire which she feared might have shown in her face.

'What on earth are you doing here?' she demanded to know.

He didn't speak for several seconds, but she could see his mind ticking over, working out what to say.

'I was at Nicole and Russell's place tonight,' he began.

'Oh, no!' Megan wailed. 'She told you, didn't she? About the paintings.'

'I know nothing about any paintings,' he said. 'What she did tell me was that you still loved me.'

'*What?* How dare she tell you that? How *dare* she?'

'She dares because she cares. As do I.'

'Oh, yes, I saw how much you cared about me when you found those pills. You have a strange way of showing you care, James Logan.'

'I'm so sorry for the way I acted that day, Megan,' he went on, his voice and expression mind-blowingly sincere.

But then, he was good at lying, wasn't he?

'I should have let you explain when you wanted to…'

Yes, you damned well should have, came the furious thought.

'My only excuse was that when I found those pills, it felt like a dreadful rerun of the past.'

Megan was totally taken aback.

'Are you saying that Jackie Foster was on the Pill, too? That she could have had children if she'd wanted to?'

'Worse than that. She pretended to try for a baby when she'd known all along that she couldn't have children at all. Even before we were married. I nearly went crazy when I found out. I thought she loved me, you see. The way I loved her.'

Megan's mouth fell open in surprise. 'You *loved* her? But I thought…' She'd thought he was incapable of love, that he'd only married that woman to have children, the way he'd married her.

'I thought I did at the time. I don't think so now, because now I know what real love feels like. It's what I feel for you, Megan. Which is why I went ape when I thought you'd only gone on our second honeymoon for revenge. It hurt me so much that I couldn't see straight.'

Megan could not trust herself to speak at that moment. Could not bring herself to trust, either. He'd said he loved her once too often.

'I wouldn't blame you if you don't believe me,' he went on. 'I wouldn't blame you if you hated me now.'

She didn't. But I *should*, she thought quite angrily.

Her back straightened, as did her shoulders. No way was she going to be a pushover this time. No way!

'Look, do you think I could come in?' he asked. 'I'm getting darned cold, standing out here.'

It *was* fresh, winter in Sydney only a couple of weeks away.

'All right,' she said grudgingly.

She led him down the hallway and into the kitchen-cum-breakfast room which ran across the back of the house. She didn't want to take him into the lounge, where she might find herself on some sofa with him. She didn't trust James not to try to take advantage of her in a sexual sense. She could not afford to trust him. Period.

'Sit down,' she said, gesturing towards the kitchen table. 'Would you like coffee, or tea?'

What I want, James thought, is for you to stop acting like I'm about to pounce on you. Sex was the last thing on his mind tonight.

'Coffee would be fine.'

He watched her busy herself making him coffee and thought of all the times she'd done that for him during their relatively short marriage. She was a natural homemaker, was Megan. The kind of sweet-natured girl a man like him might be tempted to take for granted.

Before her miscarriage, he had taken her for granted in every way.

But that was then and this was now. There would be no more taking anything for granted where the woman he loved was concerned.

'Thank you,' he said simply when she put the steaming hot mug in front of him, along with a slice of carrot cake.

'Mum's a good cook,' she said when he complimented it.

'Mum?' he said, frowning up at her. She hadn't sat down with him, having stayed standing, leaning against one of the kitchen counters with her arms crossed. 'You usually call her Mother.'

'I decided I didn't want to call my parents Mother and Father any more. Not after they were so kind and understanding to me over this. So it's Mum and Dad now,' Megan said. 'Actually, Mum's been extremely nice to me.'

'I doubt she'll be nice to me,' James muttered. 'Where are they, by the way? Your parents.'

'Gone out. It's their date night.'

'Their date night?' James could not have been more surprised. It had been no secret that Mrs Donnelly wore the trousers in the family, her husband coming over as very henpecked. He couldn't imagine their going on a romantic outing together.

'They're getting along much better,' Megan said. 'Possibly due to Dad's being a clever boy and making a lot of money.'

'But he's always been well off!' James knew this because he'd checked up on Henry Donnelly's financial status before deciding Megan was the right girl to marry.

Remembering this jabbed at his conscience. Hell on earth, what hadn't he been prepared to stoop to to protect his own pathetically bruised ego?

'Well, he's much better off now,' Megan said a touch tartly. 'So don't go thinking you can get back into my mother's good books by waving your chequebook under her nose like you did last time.'

James took this on the chin, because it was right. He had sought to influence her parents with his more than generous offer to pay for their high-society wedding. 'What time will they be home?'

Megan glanced at the kitchen wall clock, which showed eight-twenty. 'Not for a couple of hours yet. You should be long gone by the time they get home.'

James gave Megan a sharp look. He wasn't out of the woods yet, it seemed. The thought of Megan never believing that he loved her could not be tolerated. He would leave no stone unturned in the quest to win her back. But he would have to be patient. And calm. Even though he didn't feel calm. Not deep inside.

'Won't you sit down?' he suggested. 'Join me for a coffee.'

'No, thanks. I don't drink coffee after dinner in the evenings. Which you would know if you'd ever bothered to notice.'

Oh, dear, things were even worse than he'd imagined. And that was pretty bad. She sounded bitter. And cynical.

But he was to blame for that. It wasn't her natural state. She was usually very sweet.

'Then have a glass of wine, or port. I know your father keeps some port around. We shared a glass when I asked for your hand.'

'I think I'd rather keep a clear head, if you don't mind. I know how clever you are, James. You can talk your way out of just about anything. But not this time. You'll have to show your love for me with actions, rather than words.'

It took a few seconds for James to realise what she'd just said. By asking him to prove himself with actions she'd offered him a chance; a chance which, by God, he was going to grab with both hands! If Nicole was right, Megan still loved him. If that was the case, then all he had to do was what she'd asked. Prove his love with actions, not words.

Megan wished he wouldn't keep looking at her that way, as if she didn't stand a chance of resisting him. She would, and she could!

'In that case, if you'll let me,' he said, his eyes warm and caressing, 'I'd like to court you all over again. Properly this time. And for a decent span of time. We'll go out on dates till you believe that I still love you. There will be no sex. We'll just enjoy each other's company. And we'll talk.'

'Just talk?' Her face betrayed scepticism.

'You think I can't go without sex? I didn't make love to you for three whole months.'

'That's because I wouldn't let you.'

'Are you saying you would let me now? That you *want* me to make love to you?'

'Don't go twisting my words. All I'm saying is that you can't be trusted not to use sex to get your own way.'

'I promise I won't.'

'You can promise till the cows come home. That doesn't mean that you won't.'

James gritted his teeth. Brother, but she was in an extremely tough frame of mind. Defiance looked well on her, however. Her eyes were sparkling and her bottom lip pouted provocatively. A few days ago, he would have dragged her into his arms and kissed her senseless. Today, however, he had to find another way. It was perfectly obvious that one physical move on his part, and he was dead in the water.

'Look, you were the one who said I had to prove my love with actions rather than words,' he pointed out. 'Then let me do just that. Go out with me and see what happens. If I fail in any way, then you can have a divorce. I can't be fairer than that.'

Megan wasn't so sure that she wouldn't be the one to fail. How could she bear being in his company repeatedly and not giving in to the constant cravings which had possessed her on Dream Island, and which she had not forgotten? Even now, she wanted to go to him and say 'All is forgiven, darling', just so that she could feel his mouth on hers once more.

Never before had she fully understood what was meant by the expression madly in love. It would be madness to fall into his arms again. Total madness! But oh…she wanted to.

She had to get him out of here. Right now!

'I'd like to sleep on things overnight,' she said, proud of her cool tone, 'so for now, if you don't mind, I'd like you to leave. I don't want you here when my parents get home.'

'Why not?'

'I don't want to have to explain to them why I even let you in.'

James winced. They thought *that* badly of him.

'Fair enough,' he said, and stood up. 'When can I call you?'

'*I'll* call *you*. Tomorrow.'

He flashed her a look which suggested he wasn't happy with the way things had turned out. But what had he expected? That she would fall into his arms just because he said he was sorry and that he loved her? It hadn't escaped Megan that he might have worked out that throwing away her pills might have resulted in a pregnancy. That would be reason enough for him to lie to her again.

'Goodnight, James,' she said firmly. 'I'll see you out.'

She shut the front door after him, then leant against it, closing her eyes and breathing deeply. Only when she heard a car drive off did she open the door and check that he'd really gone.

He had.

At that point she began to tremble, her body finally giving way to the barrage of emotions which James's visit had evoked.

Disbelief and doubt had warred constantly with the underlying hope that maybe, just maybe, he *did* love her. He had sounded so sincere. And he'd promised to keep his hands off. And to listen to her.

The James who'd found her pills hadn't been prepared to do that. There were only two possible reasons for his change of heart. He either had come to realise that he genuinely did love her—a thought which was breathtakingly thrilling. Or he'd worked out that she might—but only might, mind you—be pregnant.

Somehow, this last idea seemed ludicrous and far-fetched. There'd been no ruthlessness in his demeanour tonight. There'd been nothing but sincerity. She really couldn't embrace such a cynical idea. It didn't feel right. No, he must love her.

Her finally accepting this fact brought an instant welling up of tears.

'Oh, James,' she sobbed, and buried her face in her hands. 'Oh, my darling…'

By the time her parents came home, Megan had washed her blotchy face and gathered herself sufficiently to tell them with seeming calm that James had come by and declared his love. They'd talked things through, she said, and were going to try again. She told them she wasn't rushing back to the marital home, but he was going to court her all over again. Her father had been impressed and her mother over the moon.

'What great news, darling!' she'd exclaimed. 'Who knows, some time next year I might be a grandmother after all?'

CHAPTER SEVENTEEN

NOT in the next nine months, Megan realised the following morning when she woke with her period. Not a heavy one. But then, she never had heavy periods on that pill.

Strangely, the arrival of evidence that she hadn't conceived brought with it a weird little wave of disappointment. In a way, this was a comforting development, showing Megan that maybe she was finally prepared to have another baby.

After a trip to the bathroom, she went downstairs to make herself a morning mug of coffee, the action reminding her of the rather nasty crack she'd made last night about James not knowing she never drank coffee after dinner. Really, she'd been very hard and unforgiving last night. A total bitch.

Guilt over her attitude sent her eyes to the kitchen wall clock. Just after eight. It wasn't too early to call James and apologise. If he could be big enough to come to her and ask forgiveness, then surely she could do the same. After all, she hadn't been entirely innocent over what had happened on Dream Island. She should never have let him think a baby was on the cards. That had been wicked of her.

Without hesitating, Megan picked up the kitchen extension and punched in her home number.

'Logan residence,' Roberta answered brightly.

'Roberta, it's Megan. Is James there?'

'No, love, he's not. He's just left for work. You could possibly catch him on his car phone.'

'No, I don't like to ring when he's driving. I'll wait till he's in the office. Oh, and, Roberta, you were right. James does love me. He came to visit me last night and we've decided to try again.'

'I knew something good must have happened. He was so chipper this morning. So when are you coming home?'

'Not just yet. Soon, perhaps. I'm playing hard-to-get.'

'That's never a bad thing where men like your James are concerned. But don't play too hard. I don't think patience is one of Mr Logan's virtues.'

Megan laughed. 'I don't think so, either. Will be in touch, Roberta. Bye.'

Megan hung up, still smiling. It was good that people like Roberta also thought James loved her. It made her feel better about believing him.

It wouldn't take her husband too long to get from Bellevue Hill into the CBD, she deduced. Half an hour at most, allowing for the traffic. Images occupied one of the top floors in an office block in Goulburn Street, right opposite a multi-storey car park. His habit was to always be in his office by eight-thirty on a weekday. She would have breakfast first, then call him on his mobile.

Twenty minutes later she was doing just that.

'Megan! How lovely to hear from you so early.'

'James, I've been thinking.'

'Yes?'

'I was horrible to you last night.'

'No, no, you were perfectly reasonable. And sensible. I admired the way you acted.'

'You did?'

'Absolutely. You are totally justified in not trusting me. Or believing me.'

'But I do. Believe you, that is.'

'What about trust?'

'That, too.'

'Oh, Megan...darling...'

He sounded all choked up, which choked her up.

'Take me out to dinner tonight,' she said huskily. 'Somewhere special and romantic.'

'You're on. Seven-thirty do?'

'Yes.'

'Great.'

'I have my period,' she blurted out, wanting to get rid of that one last shred of doubt. 'When you suddenly stop taking the Pill, you usually get a period a couple of days later. Unless, of course, you've accidentally fallen pregnant.'

'Well, that couldn't have happened, could it? I mean...we didn't have sex after I threw your pills away.'

She didn't much like his calling it having sex. 'Sperm can live for forty-eight hours, James. I would have thought you'd have known that.'

'Oh. Well, I guess I did. In theory. But I didn't think of it at the time.'

'I did.'

'Oh, Megan, I'm sorry. You must have been worried.'

'I was.'

'Megan...'

'Yes.'

'I want you to know that I love you and want you back, even if you don't want to have children.'

'I really appreciate your saying that, James. But it's all right. I do want children. In fact, getting my period today made me realise how much I do. As perverse as it sounds, I was a bit...disappointed.'

'You'll make a wonderful mother.'

'I hope so.'

'Megan, I must go, darling. I've called a meeting this

morning for an update on what happened whilst I was away. Sorry.'

'That's all right. I'll see you tonight.'

That thought satisfied her till later that morning, after she received an amazing phone call from Nathan, telling her that an American lady was in his gallery and had fallen in love with one of the paintings. The one titled *Despair*.

Two things persuaded Megan to sell it. First was the amazing offer of forty thousand dollars. Second was the fact that the woman was flying back to Los Angeles that day, meaning no one around Sydney would ever see it.

'But I want you to withdraw my other painting from sale,' she'd told Nathan. 'Please take it down and wrap it up for me. I'll be in there shortly to pick it up.'

It was during the drive to Bondi to collect her painting that Megan decided that dinner tonight was way too many hours off. She wanted to see James now. So instead of driving back to her parents' place after picking up her painting, she headed for the city, and Images.

It would be lunch-time soon, she reasoned. She would take James out for coffee and a bite to eat. And she'd tell him finally about the paintings. He'd seemed genuinely confused over her mentioning them last night. Nicole clearly hadn't said anything about them.

She was no longer angry at Nicole for telling James she still loved him. How could she be when everything was turning out so well?

Megan found a spot on the roof of the car park opposite James's building, walking briskly on her high heels to the lift, which carried her quickly to the ground floor. Five minutes later she was riding in another lift up to James's floor.

Images was unlike other advertising agencies, she'd once been told. No one was allowed to go to work looking sloppy, not even the creatives. Ripped jeans were out. Suits were in.

Or at least decent trousers and a jacket. James demanded that his staff dress well.

So when Megan pushed open the glass doors which led into the plush reception area with its picture window, she was glad that she was dressed nicely, with her hair done properly and full make-up on.

Megan didn't recognise the young but very good-looking blonde manning the front desk.

'Where's Sheryl?' she asked straight away.

'Out to lunch,' came the crisp reply. 'I'm filling in. Can I help you, ma'am?'

Clearly, she was new. Or, at least, fairly new. Megan hadn't been into Images for some time.

'I've come to see my husband,' Megan said, resenting this teenager making her feel like some middle-aged matron.

'And your husband is?'

'Mr Logan.'

Her big blue eyes widened. 'Mrs Logan! Oh. I'm so sorry. I didn't realise… I thought… I mean… Oh golly, I must have made a boo-boo. Look, I think Mr Logan is busy with someone right now.'

Megan sighed. She supposed she should have rung. But she was here now. She wasn't going to go away till she saw James, at least for a minute or two. 'Who is it, do you know? Someone important?'

The girl seemed flustered. 'I—er—I'm not sure. But his secretary told me not to put any calls through for her boss for a while.'

'It's OK, dear. I'll ask Rachel's advice before I go barging in.'

The girl seemed relieved to pass the problem on to someone else.

'Oh, yes, that would be the best. Rachel will know what to do.'

Megan made her way from Reception down the corridor

that separated the executive offices from the main working floor, which was open-plan and always a bit of a madhouse. She could hear the noise through the walls. James's rooms were at the end of the corridor, the door there first leading into his PA's office, which in turn led into his.

Rachel's office was vacant, however. It seemed she'd stepped out, more than likely to get James some of his much loved working lunch of coffee and bagels. Megan decided to sit down and wait for her return. She settled on the leather settee, the silence in the room slowly increasing her awareness of two voices coming from James's inner sanctum. She could not quite make out what they were saying but one was definitely that of a woman.

When she heard the words 'I'm so sorry', her ears pricked up. But it was the sound of the woman's sobs which sent her leaping to her feet. Who on earth was in there with James?

She had to find out. *Had* to!

James had just taken a weeping Jackie into his arms when the door to his office burst open and there stood Megan, her eyes flaring wide as she took in what must have looked like a very damning sight. For a split second she just stood there, her face a perfect picture of the wife betrayed. And then she whirled away and was gone.

James put Jackie aside and rushed after her, catching her before she'd gone too far down the hallway.

'Don't jump to conclusions,' he said, and pulled her back into Rachel's office, kicking the door shut behind him.

'You unconscionable bastard!' she spat at him, arms flailing wildly, hitting him on the chest and face.

He took the blows without flinching.

'It's not what you think!' he told her firmly. 'Let me explain.'

'No!' she screamed, her face flushed, her breathing heavy. 'I won't let you explain.'

'Then let *me* explain.'

Megan froze at the sound of Jackie Foster's voice. The last person she wanted to explain anything to her was James's ex-wife. The woman he probably still loved. Why else would he have been holding her so tenderly?

'Why should I listen to you?' Megan threw at her.

'Because by tomorrow night,' the woman replied in a rather odd but very calm voice, 'I'll probably be dead.'

Dead!

Megan stared at her. She didn't look sick. Maybe a little thin. And strained. Yes, she did look strained. Her face was pale and her eyes puffy. But, of course, she had been crying.

'I have no reason to lie to you,' Jackie continued. 'I have a malignant brain tumour. I've come home to Sydney to have a very risky operation tomorrow, which is my only hope of survival. But my chances are slim, I'm told. So I couldn't take James away from you, even if I wanted to. Which I can't, I assure you. James loves you, Megan. You and only you. He told me so less than five minutes ago. What you saw was him just being kind, and forgiving.'

Megan glanced at her husband, who nodded slowly.

'I needed his forgiveness,' Jackie went on. 'I couldn't face death without it. I wronged him terribly, you see.'

Oh, God. Megan sent James a despairing glance.

His former wife smiled a sad smile. 'It would weigh heavily on my conscience if my coming here today caused a rift between you. Please don't let it, Megan, I beg of you. Your James is a wonderful man. My biggest regret is that I didn't appreciate his full worth when I was married to him. I have no real excuse except one which has become rather clichéd. I came from a dysfunctional family, you see. *Very* dysfunctional. There were things I had to endure as a young girl, the result of which left me unable to have children. I was extremely bitter by the time I grew up. I hated all men. But then my physical beauty gave me the opportunity to make them pay. And pay. And pay. I should never have married you,

James. But I was obsessed with revenge, plus the idea of having it all, materially speaking. I hurt you, I know, and I'm very sorry. The man I'm with now…he knows the truth about me and he loves me, despite everything. He'll be with me tomorrow at the hospital. I hope I wake up for him. But if I don't, I'd like to die with a clear conscience. I already have James's forgiveness. But I would like yours as well, Megan.'

'Mine?'

'Yes. I have a suspicion that what I did might have impacted on your marriage to James. I hope not, but your reaction today makes me wonder. Don't let anyone or anything stop you from loving this man. He deserves to be loved. And he deserves to have children. He'd make a fabulous father.'

'I think so too,' Megan said, and reached for James's hand.

They exchanged glances, then loving smiles.

'That's good, then. Look, I have to be going. I have to be at the hospital by three.'

'Which hospital?' James asked.

'The Royal Prince Alfred.'

'We'll visit you tomorrow,' he said.

Jackie's eyes were so sad that Megan almost burst into tears.

'I'd rather you didn't,' Jackie said. 'I will be in good hands. Take care.'

'You too.'

'Oh, James,' Megan choked out when she was gone.

He didn't say a word. Just took her in his arms and held her close.

'I love you so much,' he murmured at long last.

Megan glanced up into his eyes and there it was, that look she'd always longed to see. Not desire. But love, true and deep.

Her sigh was one of total contentment.

CHAPTER EIGHTEEN

THE invitations for their renewal of vows went out a week later, the date set for a fortnight after that. Not a huge number of guests—only six: Nicole and Russell, Hugh and Kathryn, not long back from their rather extended honeymoon, and Megan's parents. Though of course Roberta and Bill would also be there.

The minister who'd married them agreed to come along to the house in Bellevue Hill and conduct a simple ceremony by the pool. James insisted that up till then, Megan stay on at her parents' place. He wanted to show his wife that it was her he loved. Not sex with her, or the possibility of creating a child. He took her out on dates during the intervening weeks, as he'd promised, and restricted any physical contact to a simple kiss goodnight.

Megan felt both touched and extremely grateful that she had finally found the happiness which she thought was impossible. It made her all the more determined to give James what she was sure he still wanted. A child.

So, of course, she hadn't gone back on the Pill. She really could not wait to start making love again, and hopefully make a baby.

It was a shame, then, that she woke on that important morning in June feeling sick as a dog. After vomiting for most of the morning, her mother appeared at her bedroom door with a small package in her hands.

'I think you should do this test,' she said, and handed over a home pregnancy-test kit.

'But I can't be pregnant!' Megan protested. 'I had a period.'

Her mother was nonplussed. 'I've known several women have periods when they've been pregnant. You said you were on the mini-pill, didn't you?'

'Yes.'

'Then it could have just been some break-through bleeding. Do the test and then you'll know for sure.'

Megan could not believe it when the line was blue. She almost fainted with shock, and then joy.

'It went blue!' she exclaimed as she burst from the bathroom. 'James and I are going to have a baby.'

Her mother hugged her. 'The Lord works in mysterious ways.'

'I'll have to ring him straight away and tell him.'

James was upstairs, deciding what to wear that day, when his mobile rang. 'Hello?'

'James!' Megan began breathlessly.

'Megan, darling, what's wrong?'

'Nothing's wrong. I mean, I don't feel all that well, actually. I thought I had a vomiting virus but it's nothing of the kind. I'm pregnant, James. We're going to have a baby!'

A stunned James wasn't sure what to say at first. 'Are you sure, Megan?'

'Absolutely. The test went blue. *Very* blue.'

'And…you're OK with that?'

'*OK?* I'm delirious with joy! Aren't you happy, James? I thought you'd be happy.'

'Megan, I'm so happy I could burst. But it's not just any baby I want. You do know that now, don't you? It's *our* baby that I want.'

Megan heard the worry in his voice and felt chastened. She should have told him more often that she was happy to have his baby now. 'Yes, James, I do know that. I feel exactly the same way.'

'That's good, then. But are you going to be well enough for this afternoon? Do you want me to cancel it?'

'Over my dead body.'

James grinned. 'Thatta girl. Can I tell Roberta the good news?'

'You can tell everyone.'

'I just might do that.'

'I'd better go. I think I'm going to chuck up again. See you just before two.' And she hung up.

James could not believe it when tears came into his eyes. He was going to be a father. And Megan was going to be the mother. Life could not come any better than that. He just had to tell someone. And not over the phone. Suddenly, he was running down the stairs, shouting out to Roberta.

She ran out into the foyer, wiping floury hands on her apron. 'What is it? What's happened?'

'I'm going to be a dad. Megan's pregnant!'

'Oh, Mr Logan. That's just wonderful.'

James didn't ring Russell. Or Hugh. He wanted to tell them in person. After the ceremony.

Megan felt much better by the time set down for the ceremony. She stood by smiling at James's side, holding his hand and repeating her vows to love, honour and cherish her husband. Then he did the same.

'You may kiss your wife,' the minister finally said.

Which James did, at length, making Megan glad that she was feeling so much better. By the time the kiss ended, she was very much looking forward to tonight.

Hugh immediately came forward with a broad smile on his handsome face, dear, sweet Hugh, who was nothing like his playboy reputation.

'I'm so happy for you,' he said, clasping both her hands in his.

'Here, here,' Russell concurred.

'We had some unexpected but great news this morning,' James said, a wide smile splitting his face. 'We're going to have a baby.' And he curved a tender arm around Megan's waist, pulling her close.

Nicole gave a small scream of delight, whilst all the others looked very happy for them.

'Now we can tell you *our* good news,' Nicole said.

'You're going to have a baby too!' Megan broke in, noting that Nicole's hand was resting on her slightly rounded tummy.

'Yes. A boy. Some time in October.'

'How wonderful! Congratulations,' James said, and pumped Russell's hand.

'Kathryn's up the duff too,' Hugh piped up, his chest all puffed out with pride. 'She was a week late and if you knew Kathryn, you'd know she's never late for anything. So we went to the doctor yesterday and he said to start making plans for a baby arriving around February next year.'

'Good heavens!' James exclaimed. 'All three of us are going to be fathers at the same time.'

'And mothers,' a serene-looking Kathryn pointed out.

'What's this I hear?' Janet Donnelly joined in from near by. 'You're *all* having babies?'

'Yes,' the six of them chorused.

'Well, I never! Henry, did you hear that?'

'Yes, Mother. And don't even think about it. We're too old.'

'I'm only forty-eight. I could have a change-of-life baby.'

'You wouldn't like that, dear. No more bridge. Or golf. Or long lunches with the girls.'

'You're right. Bad idea.'

'And I'm definitely too old,' Roberta said drily as she produced a tray of mouth-watering hors d'oeuvres. 'Anyone for a bite to eat? I hope I haven't slaved away in that kitchen all morning for nothing.'

They all laughed.

'Such a happy day,' Megan said to James later that night when they were curled up in each other's arms.

'Very,' James agreed.

'I can't think of anything more I could possibly want.'

'What about becoming a famous artist?'

'I might get around to that one day.'

'From what I can see,' he said, nodding towards the painting which now graced their bedroom wall, directly opposite the foot of their bed, 'you already are.'

'You really like that painting, don't you?'

Megan had given it to him the day she'd come into his office three weeks earlier. She'd told him about the sale of the other painting too, though was secretly glad he'd never got to see that one.

'Not only is it a fantastically good painting,' James said, 'but it also turns me on every time I look at it.'

Megan smiled. 'Not that you need that.'

'I might. In a few years' time. So, my love, are you going to continue painting nudes?'

'Maybe. Nathan said there's a huge market for them. Though I thought I might try more regular portraits. Would you pose for me?'

'Me?'

'You have a great face.'

'I guess I could.'

'If it's good enough, I'll enter it in the Archibald Prize for portraiture.'

'It'll be good enough,' he said confidently. 'Now, stop talking and kiss me again.'

She did.

One year later, the three friends held a joint christening day for their children. Nicole and Russell's son was called Adam.

Kathryn and Hugh's baby—a little girl—was named Isabella. And Megan and James's son—she was so glad it was a boy—was named Jonathon. Though Hugh nicknamed him Johnny Boy. And it stuck.

Jackie Foster didn't die. She lived to remarry and open an internationally successful modelling agency.

Megan went on to become one of Sydney's most sought-after portrait artists after winning the prestigious Archibald Prize with her highly original portrait of her famous husband.

He was sitting, cross-legged, in an armchair.

And yes, he was nude.

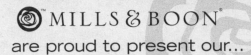

are proud to present our...

Book of the Month

Snowbound: Miracle Marriage
by Sarah Morgan from
Mills & Boon® Medical™

Confirmed bachelor Dr Daniel Buchannan is
babysitting his brother's children and needs help!
Stella, his ex-fiancée, reluctantly rescues him and,
snowbound with his makeshift family, Daniel
realises he can never let Stella go again...

Enjoy double the romance in this
great-value 2-in-1!
Snowbound: Miracle Marriage
&
Christmas Eve: Doorstep Delivery
by Sarah Morgan

Mills & Boon® Medical™
Available 4th December 2009

Something to say about our
Book of the Month?
Tell us what you think!
millsandboon.co.uk/community

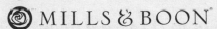

millsandboon.co.uk Community

Join Us!

The Community is the perfect place to meet and chat to kindred spirits who love books and reading as much as you do, but it's also the place to:

- Get the inside scoop from authors about their latest books
- Learn how to write a romance book with advice from our editors
- Help us to continue publishing the best in women's fiction
- Share your thoughts on the books we publish
- Befriend other users

Forums: Interact with each other as well as authors, editors and a whole host of other users worldwide.

Blogs: Every registered community member has their own blog to tell the world what they're up to and what's on their mind.

Book Challenge: We're aiming to read 5,000 books and have joined forces with The Reading Agency in our inaugural Book Challenge.

Profile Page: Showcase yourself and keep a record of your recent community activity.

Social Networking: We've added buttons at the end of every post to share via digg, Facebook, Google, Yahoo, technorati and de.licio.us.

www.millsandboon.co.uk

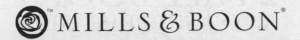

2 FREE BOOKS
AND A SURPRISE GIFT

We would like to take this opportunity to thank you for reading this Mills & Boon® book by offering you the chance to take TWO more specially selected books from the Modern™ series absolutely FREE! We're also making this offer to introduce you to the benefits of the Mills & Boon® Book Club™—

- **FREE home delivery**
- **FREE gifts and competitions**
- **FREE monthly Newsletter**
- **Exclusive Mills & Boon Book Club offers**
- **Books available before they're in the shops**

Accepting these FREE books and gift places you under no obligation to buy, you may cancel at any time, even after receiving your free books. Simply complete your details below and return the entire page to the address below. You don't even need a stamp!

YES Please send me 2 free Modern books and a surprise gift. I understand that unless you hear from me, I will receive 4 superb new books every month for just £3.19 each, postage and packing free. I am under no obligation to purchase any books and may cancel my subscription at any time. The free books and gift will be mine to keep in any case.

Ms/Mrs/Miss/Mr_____ Initials _____

Surname _____

Address _____

_____

_____ Postcode _____

Send this whole page to: Mills & Boon Book Club, Free Book Offer, FREEPOST NAT 10298, Richmond, TW9 1BR